# Deceptions of the Night

By

Angela Chapman

"Deceptions of the Night" by Angela Chapman ISBN 978-0-9845362-8-3

Book Design: Brady Jobe
Edited & Critiqued: Stephanie Chapman & Brittney Bayne

Manufacture in the United States of America

This book is dedicated to my husband and soulmate, David Chapman, because he is my rock and I love him.

# CHAPTER ONE

October 15, 2012

"Momma, where are you?" Chandy shouted into the dark, silent night. She was fourteen again and fleeing through the woods like a deer that had just heard a gunshot. "Momma, please come out. I don't want to play anymore." The faded burnt orange and brown leaves were falling from the trees like a hailstorm in a desert. One hit her in the face and she cringed. It felt more like a rock than a leaf, but when she went to brush the wet, clammy thing away, it was light as a feather. Suddenly she stopped in her tracks as she spotted the huge oak tree that she'd found mushrooms behind this past spring. "I know you are out here," she whispered as she peeked behind the tree only to find two single sunflowers peeking over a mossy rock. She glanced toward the sky—it was growing darker. The half-moon was hidden behind a distant smoky-blue cloud.

She thought she knew these woods as much as the wild critters that lived in them, but she'd never been out here after dark before. Suddenly, she was chilled to the bone. She glanced back toward her house, but it was no longer in view. "Daddy, please come back out and help me find Momma," she shouted toward the invisible house. She was furious that her dad had given up on the hide-and-seek game and went inside to shower.

"I'm over here," her mom yelled from a distance. "Come on, Chan. You can find me. Don't give up so easily."

"Where, Momma?" She took a step toward the voice. She heard her mother's soft, soothing laugh. Suddenly, Chandy was crying. She'd never heard anything that had pacified her aching heart as much as her mother's laughter just had. She had to find her. She had to see her face. She started running again. She wanted her momma more than anything in the world.

"Please, momma!" She was growing younger—she was ten and her momma was braiding her hair like an Indian girl.

Her mother laughed as she stared at Chandy in the mirror. "See sweetie...you do look like Pocahontas except you are much prettier."

Chandy climbed up on her knees on the chair and turned her head so she could admire the braid in the back. "I love it, Momma. Thank you."

All of sudden, Chandy was seven and tapping her feet as hard as she could at her dance recital. She looked toward her momma and daddy out in the audience. They were smiling proudly at her. Chandy was so thrilled she wanted to stay up on stage and tap dance all day. But the song came to end, and all the *other girls were suddenly gone off the stage. She looked toward the audience, but only her daddy was visible. Everyone in the audience had disappeared, including her momma. She was so sad—even her daddy's clapping didn't make her feel any better.*

*She was back in the woods, running like crazy, jumping over logs and branches, and screaming at the top of her lungs. "I want my momma," she cried. "Momma, don't leave me. I want to go with you. Please, Momma I am scared. Momma….Momma….Mommaaaa…..*

Chandy bolted to a sitting position in her bed. She glanced wide-eyed from side to side of her bedroom, knowing she would soon realize that it was only another nightmare. She'd had similar dreams in the last few years and wasn't surprised but amazed at the surreal feelings the dreams always left with her.

The tears glistening against her cheeks in the moonlight were real. She'd been dreaming about finding her mother for the last three years. She remembered that horrible fall day like it was yesterday.

Laura Hayes was the best mother any teenage girl could want. Chandy had been certain that there wasn't a happier family in the world. Even though she didn't have any siblings, her parents seem to love each other effortlessly. A lot of kids would probably say she was spoiled, but Chandy disagreed. She felt very loved and fortunate to have such wonderful parents.

She could still see the huge smile on her mom's face as she drove up on the four-wheeler that day—her long, dark red hair blowing freely as the wind blew dust behind her. Even at thirty-five, Chandy thought her momma was the most beautiful woman in the world. She was a fair-skinned, red-hair woman with the greenest eyes. She wasn't tall, but that didn't change her self-confidence. She kept herself in perfect shape. If she gained a pound over 120, she instantly cut back on the things that she loved like chocolate chip cookies and homemade bread. Chandy smiled, remembering all the days she'd come home after school and there would be a plate of hot cookies waiting for her.

She visualized her mom again, back on the four-wheeler. It was October 8th, Chandy's fourteenth birthday. Her father had excitedly dragged her behind the house to see a nest of baby birds. Little did she know that they were trying to surprise her with a new four-wheeler.

"Well?" her mom had asked. She slid off the seat and walked around the shiny orange four-wheeler. "Happy birthday, sweetie!"

"Happy birthday, baby girl," her dad added.

"Are you serious?" She had wanted a four-wheeler for the last two years, but every time she'd asked, she had been told she was way too young. So, eventually, she just quit asking.

"Yep, it's yours. Tell her, Scott." Laura nodded toward her husband.

"We have decided that you are mature enough for one now. But you must promise to wear a helmet at all times and prove to us that you can be responsible."

"Yes, Dad—I will!" Chandy jumped on the four-wheeler and pretended to be driving it. "Can I try it now?"

Her mom threw her head back and giggled like a teenage girl herself. "I'm pleased that you like it...but let's roast some weenies first and then we will go through all the details with you, and the *rules* that you will be required to follow."

"I will, I will, I promise! She jumped off the four-wheeler and threw her arms around her dad's neck. "Thank you!" She then hugged her mom. "You guys are the best parents ever!"

Chandy scurried toward the creek after her dad. "Can I start the fire this time?"

"You can try." Her dad winked.

"I will do it this time by myself." She'd been known to have trouble in the past and her dad always had to come to her rescue.

Chandy had loved their country home ever since they moved to Missouri five years ago. They lived on twenty wooded acres with the nearest house being over a mile away. She was glad her parents appreciated the outdoors as much as she did. Her girlfriends just didn't seem to understand nature when they would come to visit, or why Chandy would call her dogs her best friends. They were more into gossiping about boys and the latest trends in clothes and hairstyles. Chandy, on the other hand, would much rather throw on her jeans and a sweatshirt and go look for arrowheads by the creek.

She cleared her head of the so-called friends and glanced back at the four-wheeler. Her fourteenth birthday couldn't have started off any better. She sure wasn't expecting such an extravagant gift. She thought maybe she'd get a Carhartt jacket, but never did she even consider a four-wheeler.

The night had been amazing that evening—for a while anyway. They'd eaten hotdogs topped with her favorite, pickle relish, and roasted marshmallows over the blazing camp fire.

Chandy laid her head back on her pillow as she recalled every detail of her mother that day. She'd had on a pair of old Levi blue jeans and a maroon Carhartt hoodie. And she smelled so good. But that wasn't unusual, her mother always wore good-smelling lotions and perfumes—her favorite being Breathless from Victoria Secret.

Chandy closed her eyes and let her mom's image grow clearer. She'd worn an old pair of black Nike tennis shoes to play down by the fire. Her hair was red as fire truck and flowing freely down the spine of her back. Her nails had been painted maroon to match her hoodie. That particular detail always stood out the most. Chandy thought it was incredible the way her mother matched her nails with her outfits, all her accessories always matched. The gold earrings she worn that evening had a burgundy star dangling on the end. And Chandy was certain if she could have seen her socks they would have been matching also. She'd remembered glancing at her mom that evening and thinking even in her scruffy clothes how beautiful she had still looked.

But mostly she remembered how happy her mother had been and how her eyes had that special twinkle that always made Chandy feel so loved. She'd laughed and joked around with them in her soft-spoken way. It was even her mom that had suggested they play hide-and-seek. They hadn't played for years; it used to be Chandy's favorite game. Although she was certain it would be a blast, she still made her parents promise not to tell a soul they were playing the childish game. She didn't want her friends finding out or they would laugh at her for sure.

The first half hour of the game had been too easy. Her mom and dad had hidden behind the oak trees near the firepit, and Chandy had easily found them. When it was Chandy's turn to hide, she'd hid behind the shed which only took her mother about five minutes to come across her.

And then it was her dad's time to count while her and her mom hid. She could still hear her mom's voice, "I'm going out into the woods this time." Chandy wished she could go back to that very moment—she would have said, "I'll go with you." But she hadn't. Instead, she'd replied, "I'm hiding out in the ditch in front of the house. Dad will never think to look there."

"Okay, sweetie, good luck," her mom had called out before jogging into the woods.

Chandy had definitely picked a good place to hide. She waited and waited for her dad to find her, but he never did. Finally, she heard him call out. "Okay, I give. You two got me this time. Come on out."

Chandy popped up from the ditch, laughing loudly. "I was right here all along," she teased. "Mom went to the woods."

"Good one, Chan." He started toward the woods. "Come on, let's go find your mother."

Chandy shivered in her nightgown as the memories flooded her head. That was the turning point—that was when the game turned into a nightmare. Chandy now hated the game and vowed never to let her children play hide-and-seek. They had searched and searched the gloomy woods for her mom until way after dark. Her dad had yelled so much that he'd became hoarse.

Chandy's dad had been worried that she'd fallen and gotten hurt somehow, but after several hours of endless searching, he'd given up and called the police. Chandy recalled how all their friends had rushed over to help with the search. They had combed every inch of the woods, way into the night. Finally, the police broke up the search party and said it was way too dangerous for them all to be out in the woods this late at night, and they would have to continue the search in the morning.

Chandy had stayed awake all night long, worrying, with her father. All through the hours of the night, they would go outside and walk around the house calling for her.

Early in the morning, as soon as the sun peaked, the police and a crowd of fifty or more showed up to help with the search. They looked all day; they searched every corner of their property, but Chandy's mom was nowhere to be found.

Chandy's worst fear was that a wild animal had attacked her, but the police said there would have been some torn clothing or blood.

Even footprints seemed to be nonexistent. The recent dry weather had left very little to go by. The police had left the woods shaking their heads, puzzled, at what could have happened to Chandy's mom.

All the citizens in the little town of Richmond was in shock and clueless to the disappearance of Laura Hayes. She was well known in the community because she was the secretary at the local middle school.

Chandy recalled how people that she didn't even know would give her hugs and tell her they were praying for the safe return of her mom. Other families would drop off casserole dishes for her and her father.

She remembered how on the first few days unfamiliar faces would stop by to help the police with the search. Even after the search had been called off, concerned citizens would still drop by, offering their help and venturing off into the woods, in hopes of finding something the police had missed. But day after day, the volunteers grew less and less. By day fourteen, only one guy had stopped by to offer his help.

By the end of the month the media had forgotten about Laura Hayes and moved on to bash a lady bus driver for drinking and driving a school bus and putting young children at risk.

Chandy shook her head sadly. An eerie feeling crept through her bones as she focused on the half-moon staring back at her through the window. It looked exactly as it did the night her mom had disappeared. She threw her feet over the bed and moved quietly toward the window. She stared at the distant moon for the longest time before shifting her eyes to the silent woods behind the house.

There had been so many nights she had stared into the lingering trees—hoping, by some miracle, she'd see her mother running out of them.

Her eyes darted once again from side to side of the disturbing forest—even after three long years she still hadn't given up hope that she'd see her mom out there. She'd never let herself believe what her dad and the rest of the town thought—that her mom was *dead*. She was certain that her mother was still alive, and she would never believe anything different. And one day she would find her—she didn't care how long it took. One day she would be with her mom again, and she would have all the answers she was longing for. Something happened that night—something that her mom had no control of.

"I promise, Mom," she whispered toward the silent forest. "I will find you. I will never give up on finding you. I will look for you until the day I die. I love you, Mom."

CHAPTER TWO

Scott poured orange juice into a glass and took a long swallow. He glanced up as Chandy entered the kitchen. She yawned and pulled a chair out from the table.

Scott poured her a glass of orange juice and pushed it in front of her. "You look tired. Did you have another rough night?" He was aware of her recent nightmares. She'd been having them ever since her mother disappeared three years ago.

She fingered her long bangs behind her ear. "Yeah, another disturbing dream about mom. I'm exhausted."

He stared at her for a long moment, amazed at how much she looked like her mother. He imagined Laura had looked just like Chandy at the same age—the same small petite frame with the tiniest feet and hands, the long thick dark red hair, the line of freckles across her cheeks, the striking green eyes, and the dimples that melted your heart every time she laughed. *God, I miss that woman.*

He broke his trance and grabbed the cereal off the counter. He set it down in front of Chandy and then retrieved a bowl and the milk out of the fridge. "I'm sorry, sweetie. I wish there was some way I could help you to stop having those nightmares."

"It's okay, Dad. They are not as frequent as they used to be anyway."

He cringed when she called him *Dad*, not that he didn't love it when she did it—but because of the guilt he felt over it. He knew one day he would have to tell her the truth about her real father, but he didn't think she was near ready for that yet. After all, he was the only dad she'd ever known.

He sat down to read the paper as Chandy munched on her cereal, but his mind was on his absent wife again. It seemed like yesterday they were all sitting around the table having breakfast together. He'd give anything just to hold her one more time. To tell her that he loved her and always would.

He had met Laura when he was twenty-four and she'd just turned twenty-one. She was getting off the bus in Rochester, New York, and was trying to juggle a newborn baby in one arm and a suitcase in the other. She had stumbled over the bottom step and had almost gone down; he'd grabbed her arm and stopped the near disaster. She'd been so grateful and kept thanking him. He remembered how beautiful she had looked that day, but his immediate thought had been that she was married since she was holding a baby.

He thought it would be inappropriate to ask her for coffee and was about to brush her off when she'd asked if he knew of any cheap apartments for rent in the area. He thought that was a definite indication that she didn't have another man in her life. He jumped on the opportunity and asked her to join him for coffee. As they got to know each other over coffee he'd learned that she had left an abusive situation. And she had been saving her money to leave her husband as soon as the baby was born.

Scott remembered staring at her, wondering how anyone could ever abuse such a beautiful woman.

He had helped her find an apartment and hired her as his secretary at his insurance company. He was thankful he had his own business and could help her out. After a few months, they became an exclusive couple and a year later he'd proposed to her. He had fallen in love with the beautiful woman and loved her daughter as if she was his own.

Laura was the love of his life and the years with her had been the best years ever. Although they had been content in New York, they both yearned to live in the country. So, when Chandy turned ten they decided to make some changes and move to the Midwest. They fell in love with a country home in Richmond, Missouri, and had immediately relocated. Scott had been able to resume his insurance business and had done quite well.

But now, as he stared blankly down at his newspaper, he wondered if any of this would have ever happened if they would have stayed in Rochester.

Many nights he'd lie awake, wondering what could have happened to Laura that horrible night. At first, he thought it was abduction, but the police could find no evidence of any attack. During this past year, he had concluded that his long-lost Laura was gone forever. He knew if she was alive she would have found some way to contact him. And as hard as it was for him to admit it, he was certain that she was dead. If she *was* abducted, her abductor probably would have killed her by now. And if she did fall that evening and was knocked unconscious, a starving animal might have drug her off to feast.

Scott cringed—it was a horrible thought, but he was certain something horrible happened to her that night.

He felt bad because she didn't even have a family he could contact to let them know. She only had him and Chandy to grieve for her.

She'd told him that her parents were killed in a car accident and her Aunt Lisa had raised her. She said she could never contact her aunt again because she couldn't take a chance on her ex-husband finding her. She didn't like to talk about Bruce. All she ever said was that he was the most violent man she'd ever met. And he had beaten her so many times that she'd lost count. She'd feared for Chandy's life and knew she had to get away from him to save herself and her baby. She was certain if he ever found her, he would kill her.

Although Scott hadn't had much to go by except for the guy's name, Bruce Hoover, originally from Savannah, Georgia, he had still been able to locate his whereabouts after Laura disappeared. He was certain it was the same guy because he was originally from Savannah just like Laura had said. But he'd just recently remarried and was living in Florida now. Scott found him on Facebook and by the looks of his family pictures you'd never guess him to be violent. Scott had been convinced that he didn't have anything to do with Laura's disappearance. Besides he'd had an undercover detective check him out, and the guy had been on a cruise with his wife the weekend Laura had disappeared.

A horn blared outside, and Scott bounced back to reality as Chandy jumped to her feet. He knew it was her boyfriend, Kyle, picking her up for school. Scott dropped the unread newspaper to the table and stood. "Does he have to wake up the entire neighborhood?" He winked and gave her a hug. He actually was quite fond of Kyle, but he couldn't resist teasing her.

"Oh, Dad, it wasn't that loud." She laughed and grabbed her purse off the counter. "Have fun at work. See you this evening."

"Okay, sweetie. Have a good day. Tell Kyle I said to come to dinner soon. I'll make my famous taco pie that he likes so well."

"Yum, that sounds good." She swooped up her backpack with her free arm and rushed out the front door.

Scott stared after her, realizing just how far she had come since her mother had disappeared. She'd grown into a beautiful young lady—if only he could mend her broken heart. He couldn't love that girl any more if she was his very own. He decided there was no way he could ever tell her the truth about her real father. She would be devastated if she found out he wasn't her dad. He couldn't put her through anymore heartbreak right now. She'd gone through enough already.

*** 

Chandy jumped in Kyle's blue Mustang and gave him a peck on the lips. "About time—I've been waiting forever." She smiled.

"Yeah, right. You probably just crawled out of bed."

"Does it look like I did?"

Kyle laughed. "That's not what I was implying."

Chandy loved the playful relationship she had with Kyle. There was never a dull moment. And she needed that in her life right now to help keep her mind off her mom. "Yay, it's Friday! What's the plan for this evening?"

"Dustin's having a bonfire after the football game if you want to go."

"Bonfire sounds fun." She couldn't help but think of her mom with the mentioning of a bonfire. Her dad had only built a fire once since her mom had disappeared and it had been a disaster for both of them. They'd ended up sharing memorable stories and before long they were both sobbing. They couldn't even eat the hot dogs they'd roasted. They'd fed them to the dogs and went up to the house to watch a Disney movie instead.

But that had been a couple of years ago, and she was sure the bonfire wouldn't bring back any tearful memories in front of her friends. At least she hoped not anyway.

She glanced at Kyle as he waited for the light to turn green. He was so good-looking with his thick black curly hair and laughing blue eyes. The moment you looked at him, you knew he had to be a football player because of his muscular frame. And he was a darn good one too, she thought. Although she could never recall the position he played when people asked.

She sighed happily as she glanced toward a squirrel jumping from one limb to another. She couldn't believe he liked her. They had been together for over a year now. And like her dad, he was her rock. She thought she would never be happy again after her mom's disappearance, but Kyle had made her laugh again and want to continue on with life. Although she still hadn't given up on finding her mom, nor would she ever.

Kyle pulled into the nearest empty parking spot, and Chandy quickly jumped out of the car and grabbed her bag. She snatched the keys out of Kyle's hand. "I better keep these, so you don't ditch any classes today."

Kyle grabbed them back. "I don't think so, Lit Lucy, you'll be sneaking off without me."

Chandy laughed at the name calling, *Lit Lucy*. Last year for Halloween she'd dressed up as *Lucille Ball* because of her red hair she'd inherited from her mother. Ever since then she'd been stuck with the nickname '*Lit Lucy*'. She loved it mostly when Kyle called her that. She had no clue why, but it always seemed to stir some arousal in her stomach when he did. She knew she was falling hard for this guy, and she'd be crushed if he ever dumped her. If it wasn't for him and her dad, school would have been unbearable.

Not even after the disturbing dream she'd had—did she ever want to miss a day of school or a chance to be with Kyle.

*\*\**

The day was nearly over—Chandy couldn't stop glancing toward the black oval clock hanging above the door. Less than thirty minutes and the weekend would be here. Everyone had been talking all day about Dustin's bonfire. It seemed like the whole school was going over after the football game.

Mrs. Mitchell's voice interrupted her thoughts, "Put your name on the homework and pass them to the front, please."

Chandy reached in her school bag for a pencil, but her hand clasped around an unfamiliar object instead. She pulled it out and stared at it. It was a gold earring with a burgundy star dangling at the end. She stared at the earring for the longest moment—she knew she'd seen this earring before somewhere—but where?

She gasped as she dropped the earring on the desk—she suddenly remembered. She stared at the earring on her desk as if it were a snake getting ready to strike. Her mother had worn the earrings the night she'd disappeared. Chandy remembered them clearly. It was the exact same earring. She was certain of it. Her mind grew foggy as the voices around her grew further away.

She couldn't make out a word Mrs. Mitchell was saying. All she could think about was the earring. She ran her finger over the gold earring, wondering how it had got in her school bag. *Omigod,* she suddenly thought silently, *Mom?*

CHAPTER THREE

Chandy covered her ears, trying to block her father's words out.

"I know, Chan, you don't want to hear this, but you can't keep going on like this." Scott placed the dangling earring on the table in front of Chandy. "You're just torturing yourself! The other earring is probably in your jewelry box with all the other single earrings that you have lost." He pulled her hands from her ears. "Chan, I bet you have lost an earring every week for the last year." He placed his palm over her hand and squeezed. "You know I'm right."

"Dad, I'm not arguing the point that I lose a lot of earrings." Chandy picked up the earring. "This is not mine; I swear. These are the same earrings momma had on the night she disappeared. I remember how they had matched her nails and shirt," her voice cracked, "And how beautiful she'd looked." Chandy squeezed her eyes shut, fighting back the tears. It seemed like no one believed her mom was still alive anymore. Even Kyle acted like he didn't believe she could still be alive. He wouldn't argue with her, only nod, and Chandy got the impression that he was just trying to be nice. She imagined he was only feeling sorry for her.

She caught a tear with the back of her hand. "Dad, I am not imagining this." She stood, clutching the earring tightly in her hand. "Either mom put this earring in my bag to let us know she's okay or someone is playing a very sick joke on me!"

"Chan," Scott hesitated as if he was searching for the right words. "More than anything in the world, I wish it really was your mom's earring." He unfolded Chandy's finger from around the earring. "But the truth is that there's probably over thousands of earrings just like this one." He brushed away the tears running down her cheeks with his fingertips. "I'm so sorry, sweetie."

Chandy knocked his hands away. "I'm going to find her." Her voice grew louder. "I'm going to find her and prove you wrong and then everyone is going to wish they would have believed me." She spun on her heels and stormed out of the kitchen.

\*\*\*

He parked the Cadillac down a deserted, dusty gravel road, a quarter of a mile away from her house. There was an overgrown pine tree and several undergrowth bushes that were perfect for hiding his car from any passing traffic. It was a dead-end road, so it was highly unlikely any traffic would be turning down the outdated road.

He fiddled with the radio, settling on a news channel that was giving the evening's forecast: cloudy and 45 degrees for the low. He glanced toward the gloomy, darkening sky and then at his watch—8:15 p.m. He'd had worse jobs than this, but this just seemed so tedious. He drummed his fingers impatiently against the steering wheel. The money was good and would get better if the boss ever gives him the word.

He heard an owl hoot in the distance. He'd grown accustomed to his surroundings since he'd been parking in the same spot for the last couple of months. He was familiar with her boyfriend's Mustang, along with her father's Chevy Silverado.

With it being Friday night, he was certain the boyfriend would be picking her up and they would be going out for the evening. Any time now the Mustang would zoom by on the way to pick her up. It was almost the same time every Friday night. Sometimes they would go to the football game, other times out to eat. But it never failed they would go somewhere if it was the weekend.

He flipped open his briefcase that was lying on the seat next to him. He pulled out a notebook and read the few notes he had made last time. He flipped through the pictures again, Chandy Hayes, a stunning red-haired girl, Scott Hayes, her father and Kyle Weber, the girl's boyfriend.

He heard the familiar sound of the Mustang and tucked the notebook back in the briefcase. He waited until the car had passed and then started his car. He avoided turning on the headlights. He would wait and let them get a little bit of a lead and then he would tail them the rest of the night. He was certain that she hadn't suspected being followed the last few months nor had any clue what was in store for her in the near future.

***

Chandy had gone with Kyle to the bonfire but wasn't in the mood to hang out with friends. She'd asked Kyle if they could call it an early evening and she was home by 10:30p.m. She stared at her computer screen not really comprehending what she was reading from her friends on Facebook. Her mind was on her mother and the earring. This wasn't the first time something freakish had made her think that her mother was nearby. And it wasn't the first time her father hadn't believed her. He never believed her, and it hurt that he hadn't.

Her cell phone rang. It was Kyle. She smiled. "Hi Kyle, long time no see."

"Just checking on you. You seemed really distant tonight."

"I'm sorry—just thinking about my conversation with my dad earlier. He doesn't believe that the earring was my mom's!"

"Oh, I'm sorry." There was a long silence. "Why didn't you tell me this earlier?"

Chandy rolled her eyes. "Because you don't believe it either!" She recalled the last time she'd mention to him that she thought her mom might still be alive he had just nodded and hadn't said a word. "You just think I'm losing my mind, right?"

"Of course not, babe. I'm worried about you."

"I don't need anyone to worry about me. I need someone to help me find my mother. But that's not going to happen until someone believes me." Chandy sighed. "Hey, I will see you later. I need to get off here." She hung up, not waiting to hear him respond.

It was useless; no one would ever listen to her. She fought back the tears and tried to read the comments on her Facebook page. She scrolled down the page until a post caught her eye. It was a friend from school, Mandy James's. *'What tattoo would describe my personality?'* She read through the funny answers Mandy's friends had left and smiled silently. Over the years, she'd learned how to turn her anguish on and off again just like a light switch. She didn't have a choice; if she didn't, she'd be depressed in bed for days with her dad threatening to take her back to the shrink. She forgot about the earring for a second and quickly shared Mandy's post to her own Facebook page.

Within minutes, her friends were responding with witty comments:

*Dave: A fox would be appropriate for a FOX like you.* ☺

*Misty: A heart...because you have a big one.*

*Taylor: How about a paintbrush for your talent?*

Chandy smiled...she knew Taylor was being sincere since she had a knack for painting.

*Todd: A witch's broom. Lol*

*Sylvia: A glass slipper*

Chandy gasped as she stared at the last comment. She quickly glanced over her shoulder as if a ghost was standing behind her. "Omigod," she said aloud.

She jumped to her feet, letting the computer slip to the bed. Her eyes remained on the screen and the last two words that she'd read.

"No way!" There was only one person that would write *glass slipper*. Ever since she was a young child, Chandy had been fascinated with the Cinderella story. She recalled how her mom would read the story to her over and over. Chandy couldn't get enough of it. "I want to be a Cinderella," she would tell her mom. Her mom would say, "Chan, you are going to grow up to be the prettiest princess in the world, and you will have the grandest glass slippers of all."

As she grew older, the fairytale became a joke and her mom would always tease her about buying glass slippers for her birthday.

Chandy walked to her window and stared into the woods. She thought hard but was certain she'd never told any of her friends about her youth and her obsession with Cinderella. She went back to the computer and clicked on *Sylvia Storm's* name. She didn't even know she had a friend named *Sylvia*. But having over a thousand friends on Facebook, it wasn't unusual for her to have friends she didn't know. She was always accepting friends of friends of friends.

It had become a friendly competition with her classmates. The more friends you had, the more popular you seemed to be. She never ignored a friend request nor hesitated to request one from someone she might not personally know. But *Sylvia Storm* didn't ring a bell. After reviewing the profile of the girl, she realized she didn't have the slightest clue who she was nor how, they had become friends. The picture was of a slender nineteen-year-old female with thick, shoulder-length dark hair. She was certain the profile was fictional just by the way the page was set up. For one thing, the profile had been created only six months ago. If it was an actual profile, Chandy was certain she would have been on Facebook for a few years now. The trend had started years ago.

She studied the profile longer, waiting for something else unusual to jump out. Her birthday read January 24, 1995. *That was the same year I was born*, Chandy thought silently, *which would make Sylvia, seventeen, not nineteen*. "Yes," Chandy said aloud as she smacked her fist on the desk. There were too many flaws with the profile—almost intentionally, as if someone wanted it to be noticed as a fake.

There was no doubt that her mother was trying to find a way to contact her and let her know she was alive. *Two freakish incidents just don't happen like this in the same day*, she thought. She rolled over on her back and folded the pillow up under her head. She stared up at the ceiling, not caring about the cobwebs forming in the corners. The tears swelled up behind her eyelids, but this time they were from relief.

Chandy knew her mother was still alive, and she wasn't going to let anyone try to tell her otherwise. She was done trying to convince someone to believe her stories. Instead she was going to use all her energy trying to find her mom. She had to let her mother know that she was onto her and she knew exactly what she needed to do.

CHAPTER FOUR

It was just before midnight when the light went out in Chandy's room. He waited another fifteen minutes to make sure she'd fallen asleep. He fired up the Cadillac and headed back toward town. He was parked far enough away that he was certain no one from the house could hear his car.

His cell phone rang, and he reached across the seat for it. He didn't even have to look to know it would be his boss checking in with him.

"Hey, boss."

"Micky, my man, how did it go tonight?"

"Nothing new. She was home by ten-thirty. Her light has been off for about fifteen minutes. I'm headed back to the hotel now."

"And the boyfriend?"

"He dropped her off and left."

"Scott? Is he at the house too?"

"His truck was there." Micky rolled his eyes; he hated these fifty questions every night.

"Nothing unusual happened?"

"No, boring as usual. How much longer do we have to wait, boss?"

"Micky...Micky...you're surely not questioning me, are you? You know how I don't like to be doubted?"

"No, of course not. I'm sorry, boss. I'm just really tired tonight."

"Okay, Micky, go get some sleep. I will call you tomorrow."

"Good night, boss." Micky hung up and tossed the phone in the passenger seat. "Why can't I keep my damn mouth shut," he mumbled. He hated to anger the boss. He got paid damn good money to just follow a teenager around all day. He didn't know why he was complaining. *Yeah, he did*. It was boring as hell. He wanted some action. He loved living on the edge and doing things he wasn't supposed to be doing. This was too easy and not a challenge.

Before he took this job, the boss had him going around beating the shit out of people that owed him money. Now that was a lot more fun that this cracker-box-shit.

He pulled the black Cadillac into a parking space at the Motel Haven. He tossed his notebook into the glove box and climbed out of the car. He grabbed the carrying case that held his laptop from the backseat and headed toward the entrance.

*A stiff drink sure would hit the spot*, he thought. He glanced at his watch; the lounge would be open for another hour. Since tomorrow was Saturday, he knew Chandy would sleep until almost noon, so he wouldn't have to be over there too early.

His mind was made up. He was going to the lounge and unwind.

He smiled silently as he strolled up toward the bar and nodded at the cute, dark-haired bartender. She was slim but busty just the way he liked them. His mind raced—if he played his cards right, maybe he could get lucky tonight. He'd make fun conversation, tip her good, and then persuade her to go back to his room for more drinks. He was suddenly glad he'd stopped at the lounge. It had been awhile since he'd been with a woman. He didn't even want to think about his obligation and following the boring Hayes girl all around; all he could think about was satisfying his male urges.

*** 

Chandy tossed and turned most of the night. She couldn't seem to get her mother's image out of her head. She flipped over on her side and glanced toward the clock: 5:12 a.m. She sighed, threw the covers off, and jumped out of bed. It was going to be a busy day. She had a lot of research to do and figured she might as well get started on it. She grabbed some clothes and headed toward the bathroom for a quick hot shower.

As the hot water hit her in the face, she thought of her mother's past. She didn't have much to go by. Her maiden name was Peck, and she'd been married once before to a man named Bruce Hoover. Her mom and dad, Chandy's grandparents, had been killed in a car accident when her mom was a little girl. Her mother had been raised by her Aunt Lisa. Chandy tried to recall the aunt's last name but drew a blank. She remembered her middle name because her mom was named after her. It was Lisa Marie. Her last name was on the tip of her tongue. She was sure it started with a *P*.

Chandy recalled when she was around twelve, asking her mother if they could go visit her Aunt Lisa in New York. Her mother had told her that her Aunt died a few years earlier. At the time, Chandy didn't think any more about it, but now she wondered why her mother hadn't gone back to the funeral. It wasn't like she couldn't get off for work or they couldn't afford it. They weren't wealthy, but Chandy knew they were far from struggling.

Chandy dried off and slipped on her jeans and a faded red t-shirt. She quickly brushed her teeth and ran a brush through the tangles in her hair.

Her mind was full of unanswered questions as she fired up her computer. *Why wouldn't mom want to go to the funeral of the woman that had raised her?* It just didn't make sense. There had to be more to the story. Maybe her Aunt Lisa was abusive toward her mom or maybe she just didn't want the responsibility of raising her and had neglected her. Chandy's eyes grew misty. That certainly would explain why her mom never talked about her past or told any stories of growing up in New York. Chandy smacked the desk, *Lisa Marie Peterson!* Suddenly the last name came to her.

She googled the obituaries for New York and typed in the name. She knew her mother's birth had been in Grafton, New York. She had said after her parents were killed she'd went to live with her Aunt Lisa in

Troy, New York. Chandy had no clue where her Aunt Lisa was born. Her mother was an only child and her Aunt Lisa was the only living relative she had after the death of her parents.

After several *Lisa Peterson's* popped up, Chandy scrolled the list looking for one with the middle name Marie. Half-way down the page she found a *Lisa Marie Peterson.* She clicked on the name and read the obituary. She knew this couldn't be the same lady because she'd be younger than her mother, and she just died a year ago.

Chandy returned to the list and scrolled down the rest of the page. She didn't find any more *Lisa Marie Peterson's.* Puzzled, she decided to research her mother's family. Surely at one time there were more relatives. There had to be more records of her mom's family somewhere.

There had to be an obituary of her mother's parents. She knew that they were from Grafton. But once again, she came up empty-handed. She couldn't find any Peck's-living or deceased—from Grafton, New York. The town only had a little over 2,000 people in it, so she was certain they would have been listed. After a couple of hours, researching all the towns near Grafton for any obituaries for Peck's or Peterson's, she decided the library would be the best place to further her research.

She leaned back in her chair, not sure what to think. "Pictures," she said aloud. There had to be pictures somewhere. She jumped to her feet and ran down to the dining room. She opened the cabinet where all the picture albums were kept. One by one, she flipped through the pages. But all the albums were of herself with her parents. There were a couple picture albums from when her dad was young, but not one was of her mother growing up. "This is crazy." She shook her head in disbelieve.

She heard the shower door shut and knew her dad would be down shortly. She fixed a bowl of cereal as she waited. She was certain he would be able to answer some of her questions.

"Good morning, sunshine." Scott kissed Chandy on the forehead before heading to the refrigerator. "You're up early?"

Chandy had to be careful not to let her father know what she was up to. She was sure he would disapprove. She had already come up with a plan.

"I have a report on genealogy due next week, so I thought I'd get started on it."

"Oh, I didn't realize they even did that sort of thing in schools."

"Yep," She quickly changed the subject. "All I can find is your picture albums. I can't find any on mom's family." She opened a notebook and grabbed a pen. "Can you give me some names and information on mom's family?"

Scott shrugged. "I don't think I know much more than you do, sweetie." He poured orange juice in a glass. "You want some?"

"No, thanks." She scribbled the name *Peck* in her notebook and drew a circle around it. "Wasn't her mom and dad named Ruth and Ron? I can't find anything on them. Not even an obituary."

Scott glanced out the window and seemed to be lost in a thought for a moment. "I think it was Ronald and Ruthie. Try that." He grabbed a bowl out of the cabinet and sat down next to Chandy to pour the cereal in it. "You know your mom really didn't talk much about her family. She didn't even talk much about her Aunt Lisa."

"Isn't that odd? She didn't go to her aunt's funeral either. Why not?"

Scott seemed to be studying Chandy, and she hoped he wasn't suspecting anything.

"I don't know," he finally said. "She just said she wasn't that close to her."

"Do you know where her aunt was born? I can't find the obituary on her either."

"I assumed she was from Troy, New York. But I could be wrong." He finished chewing and asked, "Do you have to have all that information for the report."

Chandy figured she might be pushing too much. "No, I was just curious." She shifted her eyes back to her cereal.

"Well, I got to go into the office for a little while this morning, but I should be back by this afternoon."

"Okay. I should be home then." She finished her cereal and kissed her dad's cheek. She grabbed her keys off the counter and threw her backpack over her shoulder. "See you later."

Chandy had a sinking feeling that this research on her mom's family may be a lot harder than she thought. Her stomach did a queasy somersault. It made her mother's disappearance even more disturbing. She was determined to find the truth no matter how painful it was.

CHAPTER FIVE

Scott was concerned about Chandy probing into her mother's past. He didn't like her trying to research her family. He knew exactly why Laura hadn't gone to her aunt's funeral; she couldn't risk the chance of Bruce finding her. She claimed he would kill her if he ever found her.

Scott's main worry now was that Chandy would find out that he wasn't her real father. He massaged his temples, trying to push away the approaching headache. He knew if she ever found out he really wasn't her father, it would devastate her. She'd gone through so much these last few years; he couldn't bear to see her in any more pain.

He had also often wondered about Laura's past. It was something she never wanted to talk about. He would share stories of growing up with his family to her, but she would never do the same. He often wondered if she had a hard childhood or if there was something that she was trying to cover up. He had read some people could block out childhood memories if they were so horrible that remembering them would cause more pain. Maybe this was the case with his wife. He never really pushed her to talk about it; maybe he should have.

All she had with her when she stepped off the bus was a baby, her purse, and one suitcase. He remembered after they were married, she'd showed him a little pouch that she must have had tucked away in the suitcase.

She told him it had few keepsakes in it that she managed to save. She'd pulled out each article like it was a sacred treasure. He could still remember how she fingered each piece as if it were fine jewelry. There was a picture of a woman and a man, her birth certificate, a small seashell, a funny-looking key, which she didn't give any explanation for nor did he ask and a few other items that he couldn't remember now. He was certain that they all had a sentimental value to her, and he'd just appreciate that she'd shared that much with him.

Now he wondered about the little pouch. He was certain it was still upstairs in her jewelry box. Maybe it was time to pass it on to Chandy. She was old enough to appreciate the sentimental value that it had meant to her mom. And he was confident that is what Laura would have wanted.

With his mind made up, he quickly finished his orange juice and set the empty glass in the sink. He jogged up the steps, skipping every other one.

He pulled out the fading gray pouch that had been shoved toward the back of the jewelry box. Laura's face briefly flashed before his eyes as he headed back down the stairs. She had been so passionate about the contents of the pouch. He fought back the tears as he ran his hand across the velvet material. They say time heals everything, but he had his doubts. He didn't think he'd ever get over Laura not being in his life.

He quickly dismissed his thoughts and pushed the bag in the center of the table. He scribbled a quick note to Chandy about the pouch. He really didn't want to be present when she explored the contents. Sometimes it was just easier not to put yourself in situations where you could be vulnerable. He didn't want her to see him in an emotional state. He had to be strong for her. It would be better if he wasn't even around.

*** 

Chandy yawned as she climbed out of her car. It had been a long morning with very little luck. She was now more puzzled than ever. She had spent the whole morning at the library searching for any evidence of her mother and her family's existence.

She shook her head, baffled, as she fumbled with the door key. It was as though her mother didn't even exist. There wasn't even a birth record of her mom anywhere in the state of New York. She couldn't figure it out, but something just wasn't right. This whole situation was becoming more and more mysterious.

She glanced at her watch as she entered the house. It was nearly 2:00 P.M. She didn't see her dad's truck in the driveway and assumed he was still at the office. She slung her backpack on the table and picked up the scribbled note he had left for her.

*Chan,*
*Here's the only personal thing I have left of your mothers. She had it when I met her. She cherished this pouch and its contents. She never shared what all the tokens meant, but I am sure she would want you to have it now.*
*I will see you later.*
*Love, Dad*

Chandy snatched up the worn gray pouch and clutched it toward her chest. "Why hadn't you showed me this before?" she whispered softly. She quickly untied the vintage frayed string and dumped the contents of the pouch on the table. She spread the items out on the table. Her eyes darted from one object to the next as she tried to decide which one to examine first—the birth certificate. She needed to verify that she was spelling her mom's entire name correctly. She snatched up the birth certificate and studied the piece of paper.

*Laura Marie Peck*
*Birth: Grafton, New York, December 6, 1974 8:08 a.m.*
*Parents: Ronald and Ruthie Peck*
*Place: Cox hospital, 1900 Main, Grafton, N.Y.*
*Doctor: Sandra Moore, MD*

It was the exact details that she'd spent the entire morning searching for. She hadn't been able to find any records for Ronald and Ruthie Peck; it didn't make sense. She set the dated paper aside and pick up the photo. It was of a man and woman taken many years ago. She flipped over the picture and nothing, but a date was scribbled on the back, *1972.*

She was almost certain it had to be her grandparents that she'd never met, *Ronald and Ruthie Peck*. The only grandma and grandpa she'd ever known were her dad's parents from Buffalo, New York. They'd come to visit a handful of times since they'd moved to Missouri. Since her mother disappearance, they had only flown down once, back in 2009, right after she'd vanished. Chandy didn't consider herself close to them though. They would send birthday and Christmas gifts, but other than that she didn't have much communication with them. They would call her dad occasionally, but he didn't seem to mind the distance between him and his folks. And he had never suggested they take a trip to New York to visit them.

Chandy shifted her attention back to the picture. The photo was in color but the paper it was printed on was worn out and tattered around the edges. She could see the similarities between the woman and her mother. She was a petite, small framed lady, with reddish-brown hair, with some streaks of gray blended throughout. Her eyes were dark. Chandy couldn't make out the color. She had some freckles like her mother and herself across her cheeks and nose. But the woman didn't smile in the picture, and Chandy thought she looked sad. The man on the other hand was smiling and had his arm around the woman's waist. He was medium-height with broad shoulders and a slight beer belly gut. He wore a baseball cap that said *Chevy* across it. Chandy couldn't see any hair peeking out under the hat and imagined the man was bald.

She tried to visualize her mother's life with these two people and wondered how their car wreck had affected her mom. She was sure that her mom must have been devastated.

She did the math and knew that the picture was taken two years prior to her mother's birth. With the looks of the worn picture she was certain the date was probably accurate.

She placed the picture next to the birth certificate and ventured onto the next item. *This is more exciting than going through a Christmas stocking,* Chandy thought. She picked up a gold cross necklace and examined it for markings.  The only markings were a 10kt gold mark. No inscriptions of any kind anywhere else on it. Chandy wondered if her parents gave her the cross, or maybe, even a boyfriend. There was a seashell, a keychain with the initial L on it, her social security card, and a gold band. Chandy imagined the ring was her mother's short-term marriage to a man named Bruce Hoover. She spotted an odd-looking key and scooped it up to get a closer look. It didn't look like a normal door key or car key. She read the numbers on the back: *BOA 54231-622.* She couldn't imagine what it could go to. She was certain her mother didn't have anything hidden in the house that would need a key. If she did, her father would have discovered it by now. But she was certain that it was something important or why would her mother hang onto it all these years. *Maybe, a safe box or something somewhere,* she thought. She was determined to figure it out one way or another.

She picked up the ring again. She slipped it on and rotated it around her finger. "Bruce Hoover," she mumbled under her breath. If she had to start somewhere, she might as well start with him since she couldn't find any other information about her mother's family. Maybe Bruce could lead her in the right direction or tell her something that could help her find her mother's records. Maybe he had some of her mother's pictures.

She quickly pulled the ring off her finger and slid it into the pouch. She gathered up all the rest of the pouch contents and dropped them back into the velvet bag. She pulled the tie string closed and gathered her backpack off the table. She snatched a bottle of water out of the fridge and grabbed the bag of the chips off the counter before hurrying up to her room.

She dumped the bag on her bed and pushed the *ON* button on her computer. First, she needed to find Bruce, which she figured couldn't be too hard with all the technology updates on the computer now days. She'd remembered her mom saying he was from Savannah, Georgia and they had lived there briefly.

She'd remember her dad searching for the guy after her mother's disappearance to make sure he wasn't connected to her mom vanishing. He found out that Bruce was happily married and living in Miami, Florida. And he was on a cruise with his wife during the time of her mother's disappearance.

Chandy started searching the name Bruce Hoover in Florida, but little did she know that there would be over twenty Bruce Hoovers in Florida. She narrowed her search down to Miami and reduced it to seven names. She wished she had a middle initial to tie in with the name.

She decided to search for his birth records in Savannah and after some research she had a full name, *Bruce Gregory Hoover.*

*A piece of cake*, she thought. She went back to searching the names in Miami and finally located a Bruce G. Hoover on Appleton Street in Miami. She was certain it was the one she was looking for since the others didn't have the middle initial, *G.* She scribbled the address and phone number down. She pondered for a few minutes trying to decide what to do next. It didn't take her long to decide. She snatched up her cell phone and punched in the numbers she'd written down. After a few rings, a man answered the phone.

"Hello."

Suddenly she was taken aback and wasn't sure what to say. She wished she'd thought this through first. "Hi. Ummm, who is this?"

The man chuckled. "You called me, remember?"

Chandy stuttered over her words, "I'm sorry. Are you Bruce Gregory Hoover?"

"I am, but I'd prefer to leave the middle name out. I go by Bruce Hoover," he added with chuckle.

"I apologize," Chandy muttered. "I know you don't know me, and I am sorry for bothering you. But it is my understanding that you knew my mother. Now she is missing, and I was sort of hoping you could clear a few things up for me."

"Let's see," the man said. "You think I took your mother?" He laughed again.

"No, no, that's not what I mean. Um, I understand you were once married to my mother."

The man suddenly grew silent.

"Sir, are you still there?" Chandy asked.

"What kind of sick joke is this?"

Chandy was startled at the man's sudden accusation. "It's not a joke. I am looking for my mother, Laura Hayes, used to be Laura Peck."

"For your information, young lady, Laura Peck wasn't your mother, so what is the real reason for this call?"

Dumbfounded, Chandy continued, "My mother is Laura Hayes now, but was once Laura Peck. She married a man named Bruce Gregory Hoover from Savannah, Georgia." She was startled by the man's reaction.

The man suddenly grew calm. "I'm not sure where you are getting your information from, but I assure you, Laura Peck did not have any kids. She passed away in 1974." He sighed. "We were married for two years before cancer got her. She lived a year longer after that, but it was a tough year for her."

Stunned, Chandy was speechless.

The man continued. "I assure you, *my* Laura Peck was not your mom. She wanted children so badly." His voice quivered, "But we never got the chance to start a family."

"I am so sorry." Chandy said as her heart raced. *What the hell is going on,* she thought silently. "It looks like I have been misled and I apologize, Mr. Hoover. Um, can you tell me anything about Laura's family?"

"You mean Doty and Ralph Peck? They are still both alive and living in Savannah. They seem to be healthy right now. I hear from them every occasionally." He paused briefly. "Laura also left three other siblings behind in Savannah, which I am sure aided in helping her parents with the grief. They were very fond of Laura." He cleared his throat, "We all were."

"Doty and Ralph Peck?" she asked puzzled. "Did you ever hear her mention a Ronald and Ruthie Peck from Grafton, New York?"

"No, I don't think I have. I don't remember Laura ever mentioning those names or any relatives in New York." He hesitated. "I believe you must have the wrong Laura Peck."

"I must have. I apologize. Thank you for your time." Chandy quickly disconnected. She stared blankly at the computer screen. *None of this is making any sense and why are there so many lies floating around,* she wondered.

She threw her hands up in the air. "What the hell is going on?" She seldom cursed, but this really had her perturbed.

She flung herself on the bed and beat her fist against the pillow. *Why was this happening to her? Why was her world falling apart? Where the hell was her mother?* She sobbed uncontrollable for a good hour. Finally, the crying ceased. She sniffled a couple times and grabbed a Kleenex. Zita, her beagle, snuck into the bedroom. She tilted her head sideways and looked up at Chandy with those big brown eyes. The dog must have sensed Chandy's misery and immediately jumped into bed with her. Her dogs were one thing that could make her feel better. She wrapped her arms around Zita and scratched her stomach. She was so exhausted from the stressful day. She finally drifted off into a restless sleep.

## CHAPTER SIX

Paul puffed impatiently on his cigar as he waited for Micky to answer on the other end.

"Yeah, what's up, boss?" Micky said sleepily.

"What the hell are you doing, Mick?"

"I'm just waking up. Why? What time is it?"

"It's noon, you moron. Why aren't you following the girl?"

"Ah shit, boss. I'm sorry. I must have overslept."

"You sound like you're fucking hungover! I'm not paying you to get shitfaced every night. If you're fucking me over, I will drive out there right now and blow your fucking head off."

"No Sir," Micky stuttered. "I'm really sorry. I'm throwing my jeans on as we speak. I will be on her tail in no time. I wouldn't fuck you over. I promise you.

"You better not, you fuck head. Now get your ass over there! And I want a detailed updated report next time I call."

"Yes Sir. I'm leaving now."

Paul disconnected and smashed his cigar out in the ceramic ashtray. "Fucking asshole," he mumbled.

Any one that was familiar with the Mafia knew that Paul Gallo was no man to mess with. He stood around 6'5" tall and weighed almost 270 pounds. Paul was born to a powerful Italian Mafia leader, Gino Gallo, in 1959 in New York City. He was taught at the early age of 12 to respect his father. In doing so, he was to take no shit from anyone. He had witnessed his father killing many men that tried to outwit him. Paul's father's motto was forever etched into his head: *'If you owe the Gallo family any kind of money, you better be prepared to pay or else be prepared to die.'*

Paul's mother, Mary Gallo wasn't any less soft either. He'd witnessed her beating the crap out of one of their maids that she thought stole a bottle of pills out of the medicine cabinet. That was just the way of life for the Gallo's family.

He grew up with two brothers and one sister; both he and his brothers followed in his father's footsteps. With Paul being the oldest and his father suddenly becoming ill, Paul had easily stepped into the leadership role. If it wasn't for his responsibilities to his father here in New York, he would find that redhead bitch himself.

No one fucks over Paul Gallo and gets by with it, especially his own fucking wife. And she has the balls to take his only daughter with her. He didn't give a shit if it was an arranged marriage or not. She was his wife and he owned her. He would find Shannon Gallo if it took him the rest of his life. He'd already found his daughter and he had no doubt that *Shannon Lynn Gallo* didn't just disappear into thin air. She was bound to try to get in contact with her daughter one of these days. And when she did, he would be waiting. He would finally get his revenge and be able to show the Mafia family what happens when a wife fucks over a Gallo.

***

It was after 6:00 P.M. when Scott returned home. He hadn't planned on being gone all day but one client after another kept calling him with claims to file. He was really hoping to spend some quality time with Chandy. He imagined she'd be going out with Kyle this evening.

He opened the back door and the two dogs ran out. He waited until Zita and Ginger had done their business and then let them back inside the house. They used to have four dogs, but he'd given Cookie and Oreo to a lady in town that was looking for some friendly dog companions. It had gotten too hard to work and care for all the animals after Laura disappeared, and when the end of their chickens had died, he decided not to replace them either. It just wasn't the same any more without Laura.

He yelled up the stairs. "Chan, you up there?"

"Yeah, Dad, be down in a sec."

Scott grabbed a head of lettuce out of the refrigerator and began chopping it up. He thought at least he could make a halfway decent dinner for him and Chan.

After a few moments, Chandy came bouncing down the stairs, carrying her computer. She set the computer down on the table and fired it up. "You're not going to believe this!"

Scott swallowed dryly. He was almost scared to ask, "Did you find out anything today?"

"I did." She pulled up the list of Bruce Hoover's in Miami. "I found out that mom doesn't even exist anywhere!"

"What? What are you talking about?"

"It's true, Dad." She shook her head in disbelief. "I called Bruce Hoover. Bruce Gregory Hoover was married to Laura Peck." She pointed to the chair. "You better sit down."

Scott had never seen Chandy so shaken. He immediately pulled out the chair and sat. "Go ahead."

"His wife, Laura Peck died in 1974. And she didn't have any children."

"What? How can that be?" Scott was certain there was a mix-up.

"It's true, Dad." She pointed to the list of names. "I just now got done calling the whole list of Bruce Hoovers. I wanted to make sure that by some bizarre consequence there wasn't another Bruce Hoover married to a Laura Peck. And there's not." She sat down next to her father. "Something very strange is going on. It might have something to do with mom's disappearance."

Scott was speechless. He had been worried about Chandy finding out he wasn't her real father, but he never dreamed she wouldn't be able to find any records of her mom.

Chandy placed her hand over her dad's, "I know you don't want to hear this. But you have to believe me when I tell you this." Her eyes grew misty. "I think mom has been trying to reach me to let me know she is okay." Chandy quickly explained the Facebook comment from the night before.

"Wow. I don't know what to think." Scott stood. Maybe he had been wrong all along. *Could Chandy really be onto something?* He couldn't believe this was happening. "How could there not be a record of her? It just doesn't make sense?" He asked out loud—but more to himself. *And why the lie about Bruce Hoover? And what really happened to her that night? What had my sweet Laura been hiding?* The questions were reeling in his head. "Chan, I'm sorry I doubted you."

He pulled her close to him and hugged her. He held her at arm's length. "Maybe I've been wrong about your mother all along. There has got to be a sensible answer to all of this. I promise you, I will find out what happened to your mom one way or another."

"It's okay, Dad. I know it's not your fault. There's no way you would have known either. And why would we think mom was lying to us?" She sat back down. "Better yet, *why did* she lie to us?" She filled him in on the information about the deceased Laura Peck's parents.

Scott agreed with her. "Wow, that can't be your mom's parents. She said her parents were dead and from New York." He thought silently for a moment. "I hate to think your mother was lying to us and could have stolen someone else's identity. Why would she?" He thought of the abuse she had gone through from Chan's real father. But why hadn't she just told him the truth about her identity? He would have

53

understood, even if he didn't agree with it. He was in love with her and there was nothing that she could have shared with him that would have made him change his feelings toward her.

"We need proof though if we are going to ever know for sure. We need to get the social security number of the deceased Laura Peck. Mom's social security card is in the pouch."

"That could be a difficult task. I don't think we should let the police know about any of this until we know more." Scott wondered if this was the right time to tell Chandy about her real father. She would eventually find out anyway. He quickly decided against it. He just couldn't bring himself to break her heart. He would wait until he didn't have any other choice.

Chandy nodded. "I already checked on that, too. I found online that with some information and small fee they will send us the SSN of the deceased Laura Peck." Chandy smiled. "Did you forget that I'm going to study law when I go to college?"

Scott hadn't forgotten. "I know my little girl is so smart." He kissed her on the forehead. "Well, I am going to finish dinner and then do my own research. There are a lot of missing pieces that I need to find some answers to." He shook his head. "I am still baffled over all it."

Chandy laughed, "Oh, Dad! *Baffled?* Isn't that teenage slang?" She smiled and lifted the laptop off the table. She tucked it under her arm. "I am going to request the social security card while you are doing that."

"Okay. Are you and Kyle going out tonight?"

"I don't think so. I think I will stay home and try to make sense out of all of this."

"Sounds like a good plan. I will even make you something edible for a change." Scott was thrilled to have Chandy staying home, but he didn't say so. Rarely, did she stay at home on a Saturday night. It would be good bonding time for them and maybe they could solve this mystery.

"You know I love your cooking." She giggled and quickly added, "Well, most of the time, as long as it is not your meatloaf." Her eyes flickered with amusement and she hurried up the stairs.

"Meatloaf tomorrow night," he called out after her. He knew Chandy was telling the truth. His meatloaf was terrible. He only tried to make it once and neither one of them could eat it.

His mind raced back to Laura as he finished making the salad. He now had a small glimmer of hope that she could possibly still be alive if Chandy's intuition was right. He didn't care that Laura had lied to him. He was sure she had a good reason. He just wanted her back so badly. He had finally accepted that she was probably dead *but now* he was hopeful again. And he desperately needed that feeling right now. He wanted so much to believe that the possibility was still there and that there was a logical reason for her vanishing into thin air. He loved her so much and knew he would never find another woman he could love; like he did her.

The way she had kept her past life such a secret should have been a clue. He should have known that she was hiding something. Most couples always share their past, especially women—they love to talk about their past relationships. He should have realized it was odd that she hadn't shared anything with him, but he had been blinded by love.

His eyes filled with tears as he dried off his hands. *Oh, God, how I miss that woman.*

\*\*\*

Micky sat in his usual spot patiently waiting for something exciting to happen. It was going on 9:00 P.M and he been sitting here all day. His stomach growled with hunger. He had finished up the last of the crackers two hours ago. He was certain that she wouldn't be going out this late but didn't want to leave until the boss called.

Earlier, when he had first arrived, the girl had been gone in her own vehicle. He waited until she returned around 2:00 p.m. He decided not to share this bit of information with his boss, in fear that he might fire him.

He cranked the radio up, trying to entertain the boredom settling in. He wished he was out following the girl and her boyfriend around in his car, but the boyfriend never showed up to pick her up. And she never left the house either. This had never happened before on a Saturday night.  The boss would never believe that he had sat here all day, and she never left the house. He beat his fist on the steering wheel, debating what to do. He glanced down at his phone. Maybe he could take some pictures just in case the boss did question him about his whereabouts. He flipped the radio off; his mind was made up. He would sneak up to the house and take some pictures through the windows. That way he would have proof if the boss questioned his whereabouts.

He silently crawled out of the car and locked the doors. He briefly considered what would happen if he got caught taking the pictures. He quickly dismissed that assumption; he couldn't let his mind go there. The boss would kill him for taking such chances without his permission. He tucked his gun in the back of his jeans and silently walked toward the house.

CHAPTER SEVEN

Chandy and her dad both sat opposite each other at the kitchen table lingering over their laptops. They had been hard at it for the last three hours. Her dad had dug up her mother's driver's license and a few other documents and was trying to verify if they were official or not.

Chandy had been trying to identify the key in her mother's pouch. She flipped the key over and studied the letters and numbers again - *BOA 54231-622.* She hadn't a clue what the letters and numbers meant. She had gone through all her mother's stuff earlier and didn't find anything that needed a key. She was certain if she could find out what the key went to, it might solve a lot of the unanswered questions.

Chandy glanced toward Zita, who had suddenly started barking. She glanced toward the window and let out a terrifying scream as she jumped to her feet. "Oh my God, there's a man at the window."

Her dad jumped up and ran toward the window. By then both dogs were barking fiercely.

But the man was gone. Chandy had only seen him for a brief second. He had disappeared just as sudden as he had appeared.

"Stay put." Her dad ran to the front door and jerked it open. He ran out onto the front lawn.

Chandy briefly hesitated and followed her dad outside She wasn't about to stay inside by herself. She caught a glimpse of the backside of a man running down the road. Her dad seen him also and had ran after him down to the end of the driveway. The guy was too far down the road. Her dad stopped, screamed some profanity, and shook his fist toward the direction the man had gone.

"Go back inside," he ordered Chandy. "I'm going to check the other side of the house.

Chandy did as her father said. She knew better than to disobey her father when he took that tone with her. She chewed nervously on her fingernails as she waited for him to return. "Should we call the police?" she asked as soon as he came through the door.

"By the time the police get here the guy will be halfway to Kansas City." He locked the doors and returned to the kitchen. "I think it is time we get an alarm system though." He walked over to the window that Chandy had seen the man and looked out. "What did he look like?"

"He had a long dark beard and a stocking cap. And his eyes were creepy, like small and beady. I don't even know if they were dark or blue. He disappeared so fast, I thought I was seeing things."

"Damn bastard! I need to hide my gun downstairs somewhere."

"Dad, I'm going to be scared to death to stay here now when you are working." She couldn't stop the tears from sliding down her cheeks.

Scott wrapped his arm around her shoulder. "Don't worry, sweetie. I will call Monday morning and get someone out to install some security." His voice increased, "That creep better stay the hell away from here if he knows what is best for him, or I'll flat out shoot his ass. I'm not going to put up with any peeping Tom."

Chandy was certain her dad meant every word he said. He might come off as a business-type dad to some, but Chandy knew from stories of his past that he'd been known to fight a lot in high school, and he could hold his own ground.

She didn't quite agree with her dad's resolution. She thought the stranger was more than just a peeping Tom. There were just too many strange things going on these last couple of days.

"I think I'm going on to bed. I need to give Kyle a call first." She whistled. "Come on Zita! Here Ginger! You both can sleep with me tonight."

"Oh, he won't be back here tonight. He's already been spotted. He'll be too scared to come back here now."

"I know." Chandy forced a smile. "But I still want my girls to sleep with me and keep me company."

"Well, if it makes you feel any safer, I don't plan on going to bed for a while. I got some work to finish up."

"I'm not scared, Dad." Chandy lied. She didn't want her dad to know how scared she really was. That had totally freaked her out. "Good night." She kissed him on the cheek.

"Night, Chan. See you in the morning."

Chandy led the dogs to her bedroom. She closed the door, so the dogs couldn't venture off back down the stairs. She climbed up on the bed and sat Indian-style. She tucked the covers under her legs and called Kyle. She told him about the weirdo looking in the window and how scared she'd been.  She talked to him for almost an hour about her mom and all that she had learned. By the time she hung up, she'd almost forgotten about the earlier episode. She curled up next to Zita, turned the TV on low, and fell into a deep sleep. And the nightmares started....

*** 

"Damn it!" Micky beat on the steering wheel with his fist as he drove to the hotel. "Sonofabitch!" What the hell had he been thinking? That could have been the end of his career. The boss would have fired him for sure if he would have been caught!

His cell phone rang. "Oh fuck, that's him." There was no doubt that it was his boss. "Okay, Micky, calm down," he muttered to himself.  He let it ring a couple more times and took a deep breath. "Hey, boss."

"Where were you? Why did it take you so long to answer?" Paul demanded.

"I'm sorry, boss. I had my mouth full of crackers and was trying to chew it up," he lied.

Paul hesitated, and Micky was certain he was buying the story. He quickly continued on, "I just left her house. She didn't go anywhere tonight. I waited until her lights were out and now I'm headed back to the hotel."

"What do you mean she didn't go out? Did that boyfriend of hers come over?"

"No, he didn't come over, and she didn't go anywhere." Micky was hoping he would quit asking questions. He was scared to death to lie to him. And he sure in the hell wasn't going to volunteer the information about sneaking up to their house to take the pictures.

"Well, don't be going and getting all sauced up tonight and oversleeping again tomorrow."

"I won't," Micky said. "I'm going to grab something to eat and go back to the room and crash. I promise, boss, I will be over there before the sun comes up."

"Okay, it won't be much longer now. I need you rested and alert when the time comes."

"Yes, boss."

"Now get some sleep."

"Night boss." Micky hung up and let out a heavy sigh. He was glad that was over. He didn't plan on taking any more chances like that again or he could screw up the whole mission! He had his mind made up; from now on, he wasn't going to do anything the boss didn't tell him to do.

*Monday – 7:20 A.M.*

She stared at the reflection in the mirror. Her hair was dark and chopped off right below her ears. The only makeup she wore was heavy eyeliner underneath her eyes. She placed a Harley Davidson biker's cap on her head and tucked the loose strands of hair up inside it. She tied a red and white handkerchief around her neck and slipped into a black leather jacket.

She tossed the hair coloring box in the trash, along with her uneaten dinner from the night before. She washed off the soda bottle and tossed it in the trash. She wiped down all the counters and pulled the sheets and covers off the bed. She then peeled off the gloves she'd used to color her hair and tossed them in the white trash bag. She tied the trash bag closed and placed the hotel key on the TV. She picked up the duffle bag and the trash bag and left the room.

After tossing the bag of trash in the dumpster, she secured the duffle bag on the motorcycle and started the bike up. She slid on her dark sunglasses and casually surveyed the parking lot before climbing on the seat.

She had one more task to complete before she left town. She glanced at her watch - 7:50A.M. She knew timing was everything.

She rode over to the Quik Trip and backed her bike into a parking spot out front. The local high school was directly across the street. She could easily see the parking lot from where she was parked. She took out her cell phone and pretended to text.

She spotted the blue Mustang pulling into the parking lot, her heartbeat accelerated, and her breath quickened. She anxiously watched the couple go inside the school.

She didn't hesitate; she fired up the bike and took a deep breath. She drove across the street and pulled right up next to the Mustang. She quickly slid off the bike. She knew it wouldn't be locked. He never locked his doors. She glanced cautiously around and pulled open the door. She dropped a gray pouch in the passenger's seat and quietly shut the door.

She climbed back on the motorcycle and blinked back tears as she pulled out of the parking lot. Suddenly a familiar black Cadillac passes her, and impulsively, she jerked her head to see who was driving. She'd seen him before but couldn't quite place where. She was certain he hadn't recognized her though. She glanced in the rearview mirror as the Cadillac slowly passes the blue Mustang. It did a U-turn and headed back out of the parking lot.

*Very strange,* she thought. She headed for the highway, still puzzled by the odd behavior from the guy. And then it hit her. "Omigod" she says out loud. She suddenly remembered where she'd seen that face before. "Oh, God, please don't let this be happening again!" There was no doubt that the guy in the Cadillac was *Micky*!

CHAPTER EIGHT

Scott carried out his promise and took off work Monday to get a security system installed. His job required too much overnight travel for him not to go ahead as planned. He'd already lost his wife, and he wasn't going to take any chances with Chandy. She was the only thing he had left. He'd adopted her when she was just an infant. As far as he was concerned, he would always be her father rather he was her biological father or not.

His parents were still living but he'd never been close to his mom and dad. Even as a child he spent most his time with his grandparents. And when they passed away, it had felt like he'd lost his parents.

It wasn't that his mom and dad weren't good parents, they just weren't compassionate like his grandparents had been. His parents had worked a lot and done a lot of traveling. He would stay with his grandparents so much he eventually just moved in with them when he turned thirteen.

His grandma Hayes was the one that had read him stories, baked him cookies, and kissed his boo boos to make them better. And grandpa took him fishing and played baseball with him. He taught him how to be responsible and earn money. Scott would mow lawns for the neighbors to earn his own spending money.

All he could really remember about his mom and dad is how hard they worked. *They had money but what good is if you can't even enjoy your family*, he thought. Once a year they had gone on a *family vacation*. With his mom being a travel agent, she always got discounted travel packages Most of the time she would go with his dad because it would be during the school year. She'd also give some of her travel bonuses to her own workers as bonuses.

Scott got to the point where he really didn't look forward to the vacations. He had more fun staying at his grandparents and hanging out with his friends. After he turned sixteen he didn't even go on any more of their *family vacations*.

Bobby came around from the side of the house. "Well, Scott, I think I got you all fixed up."

"Thanks a lot for coming out on such short notice. I don't want that damn pervert coming back here peeking in our windows."

"I don't blame you." Bobby points to the front door. "Come on, I will show you how this works."

He explained the security system to Scott and started gathering up his equipment.

Scott was pleased with the system. He had gotten the top of the line security system. Although Chandy had never objected before about staying by herself while he did his traveling, he was afraid that this latest incident might cause her to be scared. Hopefully, she would feel safe. *The signs all over the yard should prevent the damn bastard from sneaking around here anymore.*

"Oh, I almost forgot I found this lighter on the other side of the house." Bobby reached in his pocket and tossed the lighter to Scott.

"Oh?"

Scott didn't smoke nor did Chandy, so he seldom bought a lighter unless they were going to grill. He examined the blue checkered lighter; it read *Gallo BBQ Brooklyn, New York* across the side of it.

"Maybe *your visitor* dropped it?" Bobby added with raised eyebrows.

Scott flips the lighter over. "No, it's not mine. I never seen it before or heard of this place." He studies the address on the other side. "Interesting!" He lifted his eyes and extended his hand out. "Thanks Bobby for everything."

"No problem. See you later."

Scott waited until Bobby had left and opened the front door to let Zita and Ginger out.

His mind was on the lighter as he entered the house. He was anxious to google search and figure out more about the BBQ joint in New York. Maybe the owner was related to someone around here. There was no doubt in his mind that it was the peeping Tom's lighter. At least now he had something to go by even though it wasn't much.

\*\*\*

Chandy tried to concentrate on what Mrs. Hager was saying about conjunctions, but her mind kept floating back to Bruce Hoover. Why would her mom tell them that he was her husband? She guessed it was possible that she had the wrong Bruce Hoover. Maybe there was another one from Savannah? She quickly dismissed that notion. There was no way there would be another Laura Peck married to a Bruce Hoover. That would be just too bizarre. Then why had her mom lied about who she was.

She was eager to get home and see if she had an email with the deceased Laura Peck's social security number. There had to be a reason why all this has happened, but for the world of her she couldn't figure out what it was.

The bell suddenly rang and Chandy nearly fell out of the chair. She'd been on edge ever since Saturday night. Every little noise made her jump. She was glad that her dad was getting the security system installed today. She was sure that would help her feel a little more secure.

She hurriedly collected the books off her desk and stuffed them into her backpack. It seemed like each class had dragged on and on. She was thrilled it was the last class of the day.

She was eager to get home and do some more research on her mother's *fictional* family.

Kyle was waiting for her by the double doors. He grabbed her hand and squeezed it. Any other time he would have given her a peck on the lips, but public display of affection wasn't allowed inside the school.

"How was Mrs. Hager's class? Did you learn anything?"

She knew Kyle was just poking fun because she hated English. She also hated the class being the last hour of the day too. She'd rather get it over early in the morning. "I learned that the bell still scares me when I'm not expecting it to ring." She grinned.

They shared their daily adventures as they walked to the car. He told her about getting locked in the gym locker room because Mr. Haines was called out on the intercom and he locked the door, not knowing that Kyle was still in there. She laughed aloud, imaging Kyle not being able to get out of the locker room. Chandy loved being around Kyle; he could always manage to make her laugh even during difficult times.

He pulled the passenger door open for her. "Get in my little English professor."

She got one leg in and froze. The gray pouch was lying in the seat. She pulled her leg back out. "What is that doing here? I didn't bring it with me." She said puzzled. She picked up the velvet pouch and quickly realized it wasn't the same pouch that she had at home. This one was new not faded like the one at home. She glanced at Kyle, "What is this?"

Kyle shrugged. "I don't know. I didn't put it there."

Her grip tightened on the pouch. She knew Kyle wouldn't play a prank like this on her. "Let's go." She glanced eagerly around the parking lot and climbed in the Mustang.

"Aren't you going to look inside it?"

"I will. Come on let's go." She just wanted to get out of there. She didn't want everyone around when she looked inside it. Her hands trembled as she clutched tightly to the pouch.

She couldn't imagine what this could possibly mean. Was someone playing a cruel joke on her? The only people that knew about the pouch at home was Kyle and her dad. She knew it hadn't been her dad. Although Kyle was known to do a few pranks here and there, she knew he would never play a cruel joke like this. He knew how seriously she took her mom disappearance.

Kyle rubbed her leg as he started the car. "You okay?"

"Yeah, I think so." She glanced down at the pouch. "Just puzzled what this could be."

"Well, how long you going to wait to find out." He flipped his blinker light on and pulled out of the parking lot.

"Okay." She quickly inhaled and exhaled slowly. "Here it goes." She untied the string and slowly opened the pouch.

"Omigod!" She pulled out a small round ceramic pill box with yellow sunflowers painted on it.

"What is it?" Kyle asked.

Chandy stared at the little pill box. A tear trickled down her cheek. "I gave this to my mom on her birthday when I was five years old." She was bewildered.

"Are you sure it is the same one?"

"Yes, I'm positive." She turned it over and ran her hand across the bottom. "See, there's my initial." She pointed to the C and snickered. "I couldn't spell my name yet."

"Is there anything else in there?"

Chandy stuck her hand in the bag. "No, that is all." Her voice cracked. "Do you know what this means." Her eyes widen. "Only my mom would have done this." She thought silently for a moment. "But why?"

"This is crazy." Kyle shook his head. "Is there anything inside the pill box?"

"Oh, I didn't think to look." She hurried and unsnapped the little box and flipped up the lid. A little piece of paper came flying out, and Chandy snatched it with her free hand. She unfolded the piece of paper and read it aloud. "19135 Sicily Avenue, N.Y., New York." She turned to Kyle. "What the hell is this? What does that mean?" Her next words came rushing out, "Do you think that is where my mom is? Maybe, she doesn't want anyone else to know but me—for some *unknown* reason."

Kyle pulled the Mustang up in front of Chandy's house. "I'm sorry I was skeptical at first. But now...I'm thinking you are onto something. But this whole thing is just so crazy!"

"I know. My dad is going to crap." She paused. "Should I tell him?"

"Why wouldn't you?"

"I don't know. I am going to look up the address first." She climbed out of the car. "Come on. Don't say anything yet."

"You're the boss." He winked and followed Chandy inside the house.

## CHAPTER NINE

She paced nervously back and forth in front of the neatly-made queen size bed. This wasn't the motel she had planned on staying at. She'd hoped to drive further away but had been on the road for only fifteen minutes when she'd on a whim pulled into the Motel Haven and booked a room. She needed to think before she made any more irrational decisions.

She was dumbfounded how Micky could have found them. "Damn you Mick, you slime bucket. You're such a friggen low life," she mumbled. Just the thought of him being in Richmond disgusted her. Micky had done a few other odd jobs for Paul and she knew what he was capable of and there wasn't anything he wouldn't do for a few dollars!

She banged her fist on the dresser. She was so frustrated. She would scream if she was certain no one would hear her. She had strategized for so long and thought she hadn't made any errors! Now she realized her plan was all screwed up. Paul had finally found them. This was horrible, and she feared the worst.

Suddenly, she knew what she had to do. It was her only choice. She grabbed her helmet and the room key. She hurried out of the room toward the front lobby.

An elderly man with an exceeding hairline and square shaped glasses setting on the ridge of his nose was standing behind the counter. He glanced up from a book as she entered the lobby. "Yes, ma'am. How can I help you?"

She kept her head bowed slightly as she always did when she had to speak to anyone. "Would you know if there is a pawn shop anywhere in the area?"

The clerk thought for a moment. "You know I think there is one downtown on the corner of 12th and Main. It's called Joe's Pawn Shop, I believe." The guy motioned with his hands as he explained the directions.

"Thank you. I appreciate it." She buckled her helmet as she exited out the door. Her hands shook as she flipped the ignition on the bike. She was terrified of what she had to, do but she didn't know any other way.

It took less than ten minutes to get to the pawn shop. She hurried into the store with no doubt what she was after.

She walked right up to the counter where the lanky, bearded man was filing papers. "Hi, I need a good pistol."

"What do you need it for?" He glanced up and continued to stuff papers in a folder. "I'm not being nosey, but we have many different ones."

"For protection, but I don't want a piece of junk." She paused. "And I'll like it to be easy to use."

The man rubbed his hand on his chin as if he was considering all his options. "I got the perfect pistol for you." He grabbed a key off the cash register and walked over to another counter full of guns. He unlocked the cabinet and pulled out a black shiny pistol. "She's a beauty and very easy to use; it is a Ruger Mark 2." He pointed to the back door. "You want to step outside I'll let you dry shoot it and get a feel of it?"

She hesitated briefly. She wasn't real comfortable with a gun, but she knew it was time for her to learn to be.

"Yes, I'd like that, please." She followed the gentleman outside, and he showed her how to load and fire the gun.

"How much?" she asked.

"Well, I had it marked at $300.00 but will let you have it for $275.00."

"Perfect. I will take it."

"You are aware you have to have a license to carry a concealed weapon?"

"Yes, I'm aware," she lied. "Paperwork is outside in my backpack. She purchased the weapon along with the ammunition and small case to carry it in. She thanked the guy and hurried outside. She slid her new toy into the backpack. This was the route she was hoping she'd never have to take, but she knew there was no other way out of this mess.

*** 

Chandy shook her head in disbelief as she stared at the computer. Although she was certain that the social security number of the deceased Laura Peck would match her mom's social security, she was still in denial that her mom would do something so dishonest. She was truly hoping that it wasn't the same and that it was just a big coincidental situation.

She slowly looked up and her gaze met Kyle's. She nodded reluctantly. This just proved her mom had lied about her whole identity. And Chandy didn't have any clue why she would do such a thing.

"I'm totally stunned. Why would my mom do such a thing?" she asked Kyle.

"I agree, it doesn't make any sense."

She pulled the card out of the pouch that had been left in Kyle's car. "I'm going to see where this is. Maybe it has something to do with this mystery."

After only a few moments of researching on the computer, she found the address she was looking for. "It's not even a residential address. It is a building with a bank along with a variety of medical offices."

Kyle shook his head. "That doesn't make any sense."

"I know," Chandy agreed.

Kyle pulled out his cell phone and turned it on. "Give me one of the phone numbers listed, and I will call and verify that it is official.

Chandy rattled off the number why Kyle pushed the numbers on his phone. She waited patiently for his reaction to the voice on the other end.

After a few moments, he lied his phone down on the desk. "Well, that is what it is, Bank of America."

"Wow! Why? This has got me so confused!" *And flustered as hell*, she wanted to scream but reframed from it.

"Are you going to tell your dad?"

"Yeah, I better. He would want to know."

Kyle reached for Chandy's hand and pulled her down next to him. He kissed her gently on the lips. "I'm sorry about all of this. I wish I had the answer for you."

"I know you do." She tried to smile. "It's not your fault." She struggled to keep the tears from falling.

"I think I will take off and give you time alone with your dad." He stood and pulled her up next to him.

Chandy didn't mind him leaving. She didn't want him to witness her getting emotional when she talked to her dad. "Okay, I will give you a call later and let you know what he says."

Kyle gave her quick peck on the cheek and spun her around. He gently massaged her shoulders. "Try not to stress over this too much. I know it is devastating, but there must be a reason for all the chaos. Your mom loved you so much. She wouldn't do all of this unless there was a good reason."

"I know." Chandy loved this guy to pieces. She wondered how she ever landed such an awesome dude. He was so darn charming and caring, all in one package. Her stomach flip-flopped as she walked Kyle to the door. She told him bye and waited until he was in his car before closing the front door.

She leaned against it and closed her eyes as the vision of her mom appeared before her. There was no doubt she was alive. She knew it now for sure.

The excitement sent chills down her spine. *Mom, I love you so much*. How she longed to tell her mother how much she missed her. She sighed and opened her eyes. She walked slowly to the kitchen as she prepared herself for the next task. She wasn't sure how her dad would react to the update on her mother. Hopefully, he would believe all the information she was about to share. But if nothing else, she hoped the one detail that he would finally believe was that *mom was still alive*!

\*\*\*

Scott looked up from his laptop as Chandy walked into the kitchen. "Hi, sweetie. I wondered when you were going to come and see me." He stood and closed his laptop, not really wanting to share the 'lighter' story with her quite yet. The incident had shaken her up enough; he didn't want to add to it by reminding her of the creep.

"What are you hungry for tonight?"

She grabbed the juice out of the fridge. "How about ice cream?" She poured some of the juice in a glass.

"You wish." He grinned and tussled her hair.

She pulled out the chair and sat. "Something happened today that you aren't going to believe."

Scott didn't like the seriousness of Chandy's voice. He feared that it had something to do with the pervert that was peeking in their windows.

"Mom was here today!"

Scott was partially relieved, but also sympathized with Chandy's words. "Chan, you have to stop."

"Wait, Dad. Here me out, please."

Scott was never one to jump to conclusions without listening first. "Okay, then." He quickly pulled out a chair and sat.

Chandy words came out rushed as she told him about the pouch and her mom's social security number belonging to the deceased Laura Peck. He listened intently as she went on to explain the research on the address that was left in the pouch.

Although he was skeptical, he could see where Chandy would take all of this very serious. His first thought was that some young punk had found out the story on Laura's disappearance and was trying to play a sick prank on Chandy and himself.

He stood and walked over to the sink. "Chan, I don't know about all of this..."

Chandy stood. "I knew you wouldn't believe me." Her voice grew louder. "You never do!"

"I didn't say I didn't believe you." Scott grabbed her hand.

"Chan, I just don't want to see you go through this again. You were devastated when this first happened and it about killed me seeing you like that. I just don't want you to go through this again and be disappointed." He rubbed her arm. "I'm so worried that someone may be playing a cruel joke."

"Dad, I've already thought about that. But nobody knows about mom and the deceased Laura Peck."

Scott thought for a moment. She did have a point. *Who would have known all of that?* "Okay, maybe you are right. But why?" he said aloud.

"I don't know, Dad. But I know we can figure this all out and find mom. I think that is what she is hoping we will do."

"Go get the pouch and let me see the address."

"Okay," Chandy quickly skipped up the stairs.

As much as he hated giving her false hope, he couldn't help but think that she may be right. Although he knew that he couldn't let himself believe that his wife could be alive, he had to stay focus and not get crazy. Just the thought that it could be possible, stirred every emotion he had in his body. Oh, God how he would love to see that woman again. "Damn, don't go there," he mumbled to himself. He'd never loved a woman like he loved her, and he would give anything to have her back in his life. And if she *really* was alive, he would find her, and he would never quit looking until he did!

CHAPTER TEN

Chandy ran down the stairs, carrying both the pouches carefully. "Omigod, Dad! I know now. I figured it out. I know what the card means." She couldn't believe she didn't think of it before. She dumped the contents of both pouches out on the table and picked up the key. "Look." She pointed to the letters and numbers imprinted on the key *BOA 54232-622.* She laid it back on the table and set the recent card right next to it. She smiled triumphantly and glanced up at her dad.

Scott shrugged. "I'm sorry, Chan. I don't get it.

"Remember, I told you this address on this card was a bank and some medical offices?"

He nodded still puzzled. "Yeah."

"Look on the key." She picked it up and held it up to the light. "BOA…. Bank of America! This key goes to Bank of America in New York. Maybe to a safe deposit box."

"Wow. I don't know what to say." He slowly sat back down. "I don't believe this." He propped his elbows on the table and rested his head on his knuckles. "Dear God, what does this mean?"

"I don't know, Dad, but we need to go to New York and find out what is in that box." Her mind was full of every emotion imaginable. But the one thing that she was certain was that her mother wanted them to find the safety deposit box. All the clues were her way of communicating with Chandy. She'd always told Chandy she'd make a good criminal defense lawyer or private investigator.

Scott frowned. "I'd love to, but we just can't drop everything and take off to New York. I got work and you got school."

Chandy knew her father was right. She thought for a moment and suddenly had an idea. "I thought you said you had a conference coming up in New York City?"

"Oh, crap, I forgot about that." He jumped to his feet and hurried over to the kitchen counter. He snatched up the calendar and brought it back to the table.

Chandy knew that calendar held her dad's entire work schedule and any extra activities he'd planned for the entire year. He even documented upcoming high school football games he wanted to attend. She waited patiently as he combed the calendar.

He smacked the table. "What do you know! It is this Friday and Saturday at the Convention Center downtown New York City."

Chandy's smile quickly faded. "Darn it! I won't be able to go. I have a big English test on Friday." She knew how Mrs. Hager was about testing. There was no making up the test unless you had a doctor's excuse or something as of importance. She was sure that Mrs. Hager wouldn't consider traveling to New

York with her father as a priority over a stupid English test. She grunted. "I hate English!"

"That's the class you struggle in already. You don't need to be missing a test," Scott added.

She knew her dad was right. "It is okay. You can go without me, but you have to promise you will call me as soon as you find out what's inside the box."

"You know I will. But please, Chan, don't get your hopes up. It may not be anything." He paused. "Heck, we might be completely wrong about the whole thing and the key might not even go there."

"Oh, Dad, I don't think we are wrong." She walked over and kissed her dad on the cheek. "You know what else I know? We are going to find *mom!* I just know we are!"

*** 

She quietly rolled the motorcycle down Hannah Road and then pushed it into a remote gully. She was certain there wouldn't be any traffic down this way, because it was a dead-end street and there weren't any houses at this end. She knew these roads like no other. She knew where every nook in the woods lead out to. After all it had been part of her plan. It had taken her months of exploring the woods and all the roads around them to figure it all out. But she had done it.

Now she climbed to the top of the hill and beamed down at the beautiful countryside. She surveyed the area as though seeing if for the very first time. Goosebumps popped up on her arms as her eyes met the driveway that led to the house that she cherished so much. This was the closest she'd allowed herself to come in three years. She had sworn she'd never risk coming back to this town and now there she stood.

She quickly shook the thought as she concentrated on her mission. She wouldn't be here now if it wasn't for *Mick the prick!*

After she'd left the pawn shop, she had returned to the school to see if Micky was anywhere near. And sure enough, he was parked a block away from the school where Kyle's Mustang was in clear view. She had feared he was following Chandy, and she'd been right.

She'd decided to hide out near the farm house until Chandy had come home from school. If Micky thought he was going to harm Chandy in any way, she would blow his fucking head off. She wasn't quite sure what his intent was, but she was sure that Paul was behind it. If Paul was behind the master plan, she was certain that Mick was up to something very shady.

She'd only been hiding up on the hill for about an hour when she had heard a car. She peered down into the rural area and saw Kyle's Mustang turning into the driveway. She immediately shifted her gaze toward the opposite end of Bonehead Road that Kyle had just been on. Just like she suspected, the Cadillac followed a short distance behind. He was following the Mustang far enough behind that Kyle and Chandy would never suspect they were being followed.

She watched the Cadillac pull into Sunset Drive, a road perpendicular from the house. She watched Micky park under the bushes. He got out of the car and walked toward the back of it. She quickly shifted her eyes the opposite direction when she realized he was going to take a leak.

She turned back just as he was climbing back in the car. She waited. She didn't know how long she had sat there and waited, but she'd made her mind up that she wasn't going anywhere until she knew what Micky's plans were. If she had to sit there all night, then that is what she would do even though it was growing chilly. It was long after dark before she heard the Cadillac's engine. She could hear it moving but Micky didn't turn on his headlights. She strained to see into the darkness. She titled her head like a dog would as if that would help her hear better. The sound of the car grew further away. Suddenly the car's beams flashed on right before the Cadillac exited on Highway B.

She glanced toward her watch. It was after ten. She'd assumed his job was over for the day. He hadn't gone near the house which sort of surprised her. She pulled her bike out of the gully and started it up. She needed to get back to the hotel and get some rest, so she could be back here in the morning. She planned on following Micky everywhere he went and if something went down, she would be there to protect Chandy.

Her original plan when she'd purchased the pistol at the pawn shop was to go to New York and kill Paul, but after some serious thought, she realized how crazy the idea had been. She'd never pull it off by herself and would probably end up getting killed. And then she would never be able to save Chandy.

Right now, the only plan she had was to follow Mick every day until she figured out what he was up to and then she would act upon it as needed. She wouldn't hesitate to shoot Micky if he got even remotely close to Chandy.

She drove down Hannah Road toward the highway as the cold air stung her face. Days weren't too bad yet on the motorcycle, but the nights were getting tougher.

She drove past the way Micky had gone just to make sure he wasn't anywhere around or planning on coming back. After not seeing the Cadillac, she was certain he'd gone in for the night.

She pulled up to a QuikTrip and grabbed some munchies to take back to the motel room. She had hardly eaten anything the last few days and her stomach was starting to hurt.

As she entered the motel parking lot she scanned the area making sure that no one was sitting in their cars. She pulled to the very back of the motel and parked her bike—just a simple precaution that she always took. She grabbed her backpack and walked around to the side of the hotel where her room was. She had the key in her door and was turning it when she heard a familiar car. She glanced up just as the Cadillac's headlights pulled into a parking place. "Oh shit!" she whispered and quickly slipped into the room. She quickly shut the door and bolted it. *Sonofabitch! Is he following me? Did he recognize me? Crap, maybe he knows I was following him*. Her body trembled. She set down her gear and pulled the pistol out. Without turning on any lights, she made her way to the window. She peeked between the flowered curtains and seen him just as he used his key to a room a few doors down.

She let out a sigh. She was flabbergasted that he was staying in the same motel but relieved he wasn't there looking for her.

She flipped on the light and sat down on the bed to eat. This would make it really easy to keep tabs on him, she thought, but also, she'd have to be careful because this would make it easy for him to discover her too!

***

Scott stayed up late, booking a hotel room and making flight reservations. He knew he'd have plenty of free time. The meetings never lasted long, and the trips usually turned into mini vacations.

Long after Chandy had gone to bed he'd sat at the table, pondering over the recent episodes that had happened. As much as he wanted to believe the possibility that his wife may be alive, he didn't want to feel the disappointment if it was all a big hoax. He couldn't imagine why Laura had lied to him about her identity. She had already told him she was hiding from her ex-husband, so why would she lie about anything else? He rubbed his forehead as he stared at the card Chandy had found in the pouch. He then picked up the key and verified that the markings were accurate. They said BOA which very well could mean Bank of America. It all did make sense except for all the lies and the secrecy. *Could Laura have gotten mixed up in something she was ashamed of and couldn't tell him?*

He pulled out the lighter and tossed it on the table with the rest of the treasure. Scott wondered if the guy peeking in the window had anything to do with the big mess.

He'd looked up *Gallo's BQ* that was written on the lighter. It was in a nice area in Brooklyn. He thought he might just have to eat lunch there one day while he was in New York.

Then there was Chandy that he had to worry about while he was gone. The thought of leaving her by herself all weekend with that creep running around bothered him terribly. As much as he didn't want to start a routine of Kyle staying overnight, he was half tempted to ask him to stay with her.

He knew it wasn't right. But all he could do is tell Chandy that he had to sleep in the spare bedroom, rather they would abide by it, he would never know.

Of course, he came to the conclusion a long time ago that it was possible she was already sexual active. Lord knows he was at that age.

Not much he could do about it, but he just didn't want to give her the impression that he thought it was okay.

He knew Kyle's mom and dad, Virgil and Betty Adams, they were clients of his. They were good folks and Scott was sure if he talked to them first they would understand his concern. They were crazy about Chandy, so he was certain they wouldn't mind Kyle staying with her for safety reasons.

He yawned and glanced at the clock on the stove. It was after midnight. "Come on, girls," he yelled at the dogs. He let them outside and waited while they did their business. He then locked up the doors and headed to his bedroom. He knew five o'clock would come around fast and needed to get some rest.

Scott crawled into his bed and once again thought of Laura. It had become a nightly routine that he couldn't quite shake. Every night he visualized Laura the last time he had saw her asleep in the bed. It was the morning she'd disappeared. He'd woken up before the alarm had gone off and he'd hurriedly turned it off, so it wouldn't wake her. He thought he'd let her sleep in while he showered. He'd glanced down at her and remembered thinking how lucky he was to have such a beautiful, caring wife.

As he closed his eyes her image passed again before him. It was a memory that always seemed to comfort him right before he went to sleep. He knew he didn't want to go the rest of his life by himself. He planned on dating again one of these days, but not for a long time. At least, not if Chandy lived with him.

But if there was a possibility of Laura being alive, he had no desire for another woman. He'd wait the rest of his life for his wife if there was a chance she was out there somewhere. He didn't care what she had done wrong in her past he would forgive her and protect her like he'd promised to do. And with that thought Scott fell into a deep sleep.

## CHAPTER ELEVEN

Chandy woke up earlier than usual for a change. She had a tingling feeling in the pit of her stomach, and she knew exactly why. Although it was only Tuesday, it felt like Friday. She could hardly wait for her dad to go to New York to see what he could find out about her mom. This was going to be the longest week ever.

She jumped out of bed and fired up her computer. She quickly scanned Sylvia Storm's page to see if she had any updates. This was something she done on a regular basis now since *Sylvia* had left the comment on her wall the other night. There wasn't anything. She checked her own wall, but nothing there either.

Chandy turned the computer off and gathered her clothes for her shower. She was sure her dad was already done with his and probably downstairs cooking breakfast. Something he'd always done even when mom was with them. He loved cooking breakfast. During the week, it was never anything fancy but on weekends he used to go all out. They would have bacon, eggs, pancakes, and biscuits with gravy—the whole works. She would usually be full all day after eating one of her dad's weekend breakfasts.

He didn't cook quite as much since her mom had disappeared. But he still enjoyed cooking bacon and eggs occasionally during the week. Other times they would have hot biscuits and jelly; some mornings Chandy preferred just cold cereal and milk.

She showered and got dressed. The aroma of fresh coffee and bacon frying flowed through the house. Suddenly she was starving and glad her dad was cooking.

Her father was setting the bacon and eggs on the table as she entered the kitchen. He glanced up. "Good morning, princess."

"Good morning, Dad. It smells yummy and I'm hungry."

"Dig in. I'll have some toast ready in a second."

Chandy hurriedly sat down and filled her plate. She didn't drink coffee often but, every once in a while, she liked it. This morning she thought she could use a little stimulation to get through the long, boring school day. She poured the steaming liquid into a cup and sprinkled sugar into it. After stirring it with her spoon, she took a sip of the hot coffee. "I'm going in early today to help Marcus with his art project."

"Oh?" Scott set a piece of buttered toast on Chandy's plate. He pulled up a chair next to her and sat down. "No Kyle this morning?"

"No, I'm driving. I told Marcus I'd be there early. He was going in at 7:00, I think."

Scott glanced toward the clock on the stove. "It's almost 7:00 now."

"I know—I told him I'd be a few minutes late."

"Well, then I better get right to the point."

Chandy looked up from her plate. "What point?"

"I did some thinking and while I'm gone this weekend, I would feel better if maybe you had Kyle stay here with you." He grinned and shook his finger at her. "But he sleeps in the spare room."

Chandy laughed. "You mean you trust me?"

"Well, I'd like to think that I can."

She finished chewing. "Don't worry. You can trust me, Dad. That will be fine." She finished the coffee and stood. "Although, I really don't mind staying by myself. If it is that guy that was peeking in the window that you are concerned about, I'm not scared any more—now that you got the security system. I can take care of myself. Besides I got my girls." She patted Ginger and Zita's head as she strolled by.

"I know you can. It will just make me feel better," he said.

Chandy slipped on her jacket. "Sure, Dad, if that is what you want. I will ask him today."

"Why don't you wait? I would like to speak to Betty and Virgil first about the situation."

"Okay, whatever." She scooped up her bag and purse. "I gotta get going."

"Okay, sweetie, have a good day. See you tonight." Scott walked her to the door and opened it.

"Bye Dad." She hurried to her Honda Civic and climbed in. She felt like she hadn't been in her own car for days. She started the car and thought of her dad as she waited for it to warm up. She thought it was cute how he was being so overprotective of her. She could tell the sudden increase in safeguarding her since her mother disappeared. She really didn't mind though. It just proved how much he loved her.

She reached the end of her driveway and turned on Bonehill Road just as the sun hit her in the eyes. She squinted and pulled down the visor. A big black car was coming toward her and because of the narrowness of the road she had to hug the side tightly for him to pass. "Come on mister. Get on your side," She mumbled as she glanced toward him. Her adrenaline suddenly amplified as her eyes locked with the beady-eyed character. "Omigod," she said loudly. It was the same guy that she'd seen peeping in their window. He was still wearing the funky blue stocking cap. *What the hell was he doing on her road again? That stupid ass jerk!* She hurriedly shifted her eyes toward the road. She didn't want him to know that she knew it was him. Although once again, she couldn't tell the color of his eyes, but she would recognize those piercing malicious eyes anywhere. They were so creepy!

She continued to glance in her rearview mirror until he was no longer in view. She snatched up her phone to call her dad. But after a few seconds, she decided against it. She knew if he knew that man was anywhere nearby, he would cancel his trip for the weekend. And she just couldn't risk that. She had to know what was in the safe deposit box at the bank or it was going to drive her crazy. Her mind was made, she wouldn't tell her dad about the occurrence with the peculiar man.

"Fuck! Sonofabitch!" Micky banged his fist into the console. *What the hell was she doing leaving the house so early? She never leaves this early!*

There was no doubt she saw him. She looked right at him and seemed to be sizing him up and down. *Does she know? Did she see what I looked like the other night?* He hadn't thought she had but maybe she did. "Shit!" He drove on passed the street he usually turned down. He knew another way out rather than turning around and following her. He couldn't take that chance now. *Paul is going to kill me if I fuck up this mission,* he thought.

His cell phone rang. "No, not now. Call me later," he yelled at the ringing phone. There was no doubt in his mind who was on the other end of his cell phone, but he couldn't decide rather to tell him about Chandy? But then again, his boss didn't know about him peeking in the windows and getting caught so maybe he wouldn't think anything of it. He snatched his phone up. "Hey, boss!"

"You up and about, Micky, my man?"

"Yes, Sir. But Chandy just passed me in her car." He hadn't planned on saying it so bluntly, it just slipped out.

"What the hell you are talking about, Mick?"

"I was on my way to my usual spot. Her boyfriend always picks her up a little bit before eight and for some reason she took her own car early to school, I guess."

"Well, she doesn't know who you are. So, what's the problem? Just turn around and get on her ass!"

"I know," he stuttered. "It just caught me by surprise."

"Just don't make it a habit and get back on her trail. I will call you this evening. I don't want any fuck-up's today! Do you hear?"

"Yes, Sir." Micky flipped his middle finger at the phone and hung up. "Why don't you come up here and follow this boring ass girl around all day and night and see how you like it," he mumbled to the silent phone. "Maybe I should just kidnap her and make you pay me a bunch of money to get her back." *Damn, why hadn't I thought of that before? Surprisingly, my brain must have survived all the drug abuse after all,* he thought amusingly. *It really was a good idea. And no doubt Paul had plenty of money and could pay a high ransomed. He could probably purchase half of New York with all the money he had.* Micky shrugged; it didn't matter to him that it was *dirty money.*

He laughed and quickly dismissed the silly notion. He knew Paul would hunt him down and kill him with his bare hands. No way was he going to mess with Paul Gallo. Plus, most of the mafia in New York knew and respected Paul. *None of them would hesitate to help him butcher me! I'm not going there,* he thought.

He caught up with Chandy just as she pulled into the high school. He was sure to keep his distance this time, so she didn't recognize the car.

He parked in the same spot he always did while classes were in session. He'd snooze for about an hour and then go get something to eat. He would come back to the same spot and wait until school was out. *Same old fucking thing every day!* He sighed. But the money was good, so he'd stick with it. Besides, Paul had said it wouldn't be much longer and he would get do some exciting work. He could hardly wait!

\*\*\*

She'd left the motel before daylight, gassed up her bike, and grabbed some snacks and bottled water before heading up to her new spot on the hill. She was glad she'd come early because Chandy had left the house before Micky ever got there.

Chandy had taken her own car to school rather than waiting for Kyle to pick her up. It was earlier than usual for Chandy to go to school, but she knew that wasn't unusual. They were always having school activities before and after school.

She was glad Micky wasn't there. She debated rather to go to the school or wait for her to return home. She quickly decided she needed to get to the school and make sure Chandy got there safely.

She started up the motorcycle and headed toward the school. She wouldn't get as close to the school as she did yesterday. She couldn't take that chance. She'd just drive by and see if Chandy's car was there and then go back to the hotel and wait for school to be out.

As she neared the school, she slowed down. She was relieved to see the familiar Honda Civic parked right next to Kyle's Mustang. She went on pass the school, looking for the black Cadillac. She didn't see the car anywhere around and assumed Micky was taking a break until school got out.

She spun her bike around and headed out of town, toward the motel. She needed to stay under covered as much as possible. She couldn't risk too many people seeing her. Apparently, Micky had the same idea. She was sure Paul had set everything up because Micky wasn't that bright. She knew if she got the chance to outwit the idiot she would. And if she had to shoot him to do so, she wouldn't hesitate to do it either.

.

CHAPTER TWELVE

*Friday, Oct. 23, 2012*

Chandy couldn't believe it was finally Friday. It had been the longest week ever. She jumped out of bed even though it wasn't even 5:00 A.M. yet. She knew her dad needed to be at the airport by 8:00 A.M. and she wasn't going to take any chances of him missing his plane. She wanted to make sure he was up and getting ready.

She booted up her computer just as she heard the shower running. She underestimated her dad. He was already up and about.

She clicked on the Facebook icon and waited for it to upload. She clicked her notifications and didn't have anything. She typed in Sylvia Storm's name to go to her page.

"Yay, she's been on!" There was a post on Sylvia's wall.

She quickly read the written words.

*Never trust a man with a stray puppy. He will break your heart.*

"Omigod!" She stared in disbelief at the computer. There was no doubt that her mother had wrote it. Her mom used to preach to her all the time about how strange men might try to get her to come over to their car and see the puppy they found. *It has to be her. But why the heck would she write this? Why is she being so secretive about everything?*

She glanced away from the computer as doubt suddenly overwhelmed her. *Maybe Sylvia wasn't her mom.* There had to be lots of mothers that warn their daughters on how strangers lured their kids into cars. Maybe she'd fantasized for so long about her mother being alive that somehow, she had created the entire illusion in her head. A tear slipped down her cheek. She just didn't know what was real anymore.

She thought about how crushed she would be if her dad called and said that the key didn't go to any safe deposit box and that she'd been wrong about everything.

Chandy heard the shower shut off. "No, I can't be negative," she said under her breath. Her mom always told her to follow her gut. And she was certain that she was right about her mom. She couldn't let herself think differently.

Her adrenaline increased again, and she grabbed her clothes to shower. She was certain her dad would insist on making breakfast for her no matter how late he was running. She planned on taking a quick shower and getting downstairs. She thought she could load up his suitcase for him while he was cooking. She was going to get him out that door and to the airport if she had to drive him herself.

Chandy was approaching the bottom of the stairs just as her dad was sitting pancakes on the table. "Dad, I told you I'd eat cold cereal today."

"I'm running ahead of schedule, so I whipped you up some of my famous pumpkin pancakes."

"Yum. Thanks, Dad." She sat down at the table. "But you need to be at the airport early."

Scott handed Chandy the syrup. "Now how long have I been making these trips, Chan?"

She knew he was right. "I'm sorry, Dad." She grinned. "I'm just really nervous."

"It's okay, sweetie. I know you are." He finished chewing and added. "Just relax." He sipped his coffee. "I'll have all weekend. These meetings don't last any time."

"And you promise you will call me as soon as you know something?"

"I promise." He set his fork down. "And you promise to call me if you need anything, right?" He pushed a piece of paper. "Here is the Holiday Inn phone number and the location along with the meeting place address. I've put all the phone numbers right together." He tapped his index finger on the paper.

"Dad, I will be fine. I will be hanging out with Kyle most of the time." She was glad she hadn't told him about the man she'd seen earlier in the week. She was sure he would have cancelled the trip.

"And don't forget to set the alarm when you leave and again when you get inside."

"I will, Dad." She finished eating and carried her plate over to the sink. "I'll take your suitcase out while you finish eating."

Scott stuffed the last bite in his mouth and stood. "I'm done now. Chill princess, I'll get it." He smiled and tousled Chandy's hair. "I got plenty of time before I have to leave." He opened the door for Zita and Ginger to go outside.

"Sorry." She rolled her eyes toward the ceiling. "Okay, I will leave you be. I'm going to go watch the weather. Yell at me when you are ready to go."

"Don't worry. I will."

Chandy went into the living room to watch the news and wait for her Dad to yell at her.

She had some homework that she needed to catch up on while she waited.

Finally, after what seem like an eternity her dad yelled that he had to get going. She walked him out to the car and gave him a hug. "I will be out of class by 3:00. Don't forget to call and let me know something—even if you don't know anything!"

"I will, I will. Now get back in the house and wait for Kyle." He glanced toward the sky. "Sun is not even all the way out yet."

"Okay. Bye Dad. I love you." She walked backwards toward the front door, blowing kisses as she did.

"I love you too, Chan. Be careful and stay out of trouble!" He winked and climbed into his truck.

\*\*\*

Scott waited for the seat belt light to go off before he stood and retrieved his briefcase from the storage case above his head. The flight had been smooth and seemed to go by fairly fast. He'd read the upcoming schedule for the weekend and dozed some.

He had to be at the initial meeting at noon to go over the weekend details and then he would be free the rest of the day to do as he pleased. He figured he would go by the bank first thing after the briefing and then play it by ear after that.

Scott checked his watch and thought about Chandy; she should be sitting in class by now. He was trying not to worry about her, but it was hard not to. He had taken many trips away from home and left her alone, but he'd never experienced a peeping Tom before either. He hoped he didn't regret his decision in going.

He checked into the hotel first thing to dump off his luggage and then flagged down a taxi to take him to the conference center.

He gave the driver the conference center address and asked him about the address of the Bank of America. Luckily, it wasn't too far from the center, and he could head that way as soon as the meeting was over.

Scott patted his pants pocket to make sure the key was still there. He knew it would be since he'd already checked it this morning because Chandy had insisted on it. He smiled at the thought of how she was always mothering him. Scott was already missing her.

He pulled his briefcase on his lap, flipped the latched, and doubled checked to see if the folder was still on top. He hadn't told Chandy about having to get a court order. She'd just assume anyone could walk into a bank and try the key out in the safe deposit box. She knew he had all her mom's forms of identification, but she hadn't known about the court order. Scott had called the bank first and found out that he had to have one. He'd called his buddy, Tyler Smith, from Kansas City. He'd met Tyler at a convention a few years back. They had gone down to the lounge after the convention and had drinks together and shared laughs. They'd been good friends ever since. Tyler owned a law firm and didn't hesitate to get Scott the documentation that he needed.

Scott closed his case and latched it just as the cab driver pulled up to the center. He thanked him and gave him a tip.

He'd forgotten how busy New York City was. There were people bustling to their destinations everywhere. If he didn't know better, he'd swear that half of America lived in this city.

Scott maneuvered his way into the conference center. It was 11:55 A.M. He'd barely made it. He greeted a few guys that he knew, promising them he'd meet up with them later tonight for drinks in the lounge. He grabbed an empty seat just as the host started speaking.

After a few jokes and helpful tips on ways to get around in the city, the host explained the times they would be expected back at the conference center and what they would be learning during the weekend.

Finally, after an hour, the elderly gentleman dismissed them for the day. The guy hurried and added, "Don't forget 9:00 a.m. sharp in the morning. Don't stay out late tonight and oversleep."

Scott heard a few snide remarks and laughter as he exited out the door.

His adrenaline increased as he thought about his next stop. He didn't think about the possibilities of what was inside Laura's safe deposit box, *if there was even one*. He hadn't gotten his hopes up until now. But he suddenly realized how disappointed he would be if this whole thing was a big hoax.

Scott flagged down a taxi and crawled inside. He hadn't prayed for a long time but suddenly he prayed like crazy as they drove toward the bank.

\*\*\*

Micky called his boss and drummed his thumbs on the steering wheel as he waited for his boss to answer. He was certain that he had news that his boss would want to hear.

"Mick, my man, what's up?" Paul said on the other end.

"You're not going to believe this, boss?"

"Shit!" He grunted. "What did you do now? You better not of fucked up!"

Micky didn't know a man that could change from being pleasant one moment to an arrogant bastard in five seconds like his boss could. "I didn't do a thing, boss. I just have some information that I thought you would like to have."

"Okay, I'm listening. Spill it!"

Micky flipped his middle finger at the phone and reluctantly  continued, "Well, I thought I'd go early to the house today in case she left early for school again." He paused long enough to make sure the boss wasn't going to interrupt again. "Anyway, Chandy didn't leave early this morning, but her father did. *And* he had a suitcase."

There was a long pause. Suddenly Paul added. "I'm going to call his work and pretend I'm a client. I'll find out where he's headed."

"What do you want me to do?"

"She went to school like always, right?"

"Yeah, her boyfriend picked her up," Micky said.

"Then keep following her. We may have to speed up the plan real fast!"

Paul's word perked Micky's interest. "Okay, boss." He liked the sound of that. It looked like things could get interesting real soon! He couldn't be more pleased. *Finally—let the fun begin!*

## CHAPTER THIRTEEN

The polite, classic lady at the bank led Scott back to the vault. He hoped the woman couldn't tell how nervous he was. He was sure his voice had been shaking when he'd spoken. He hadn't gone into any detail; he'd just showed her the necessary paper work.

He was thrilled when she'd confirmed there was a box under Laura Peck's name.

They entered the vault and the lady located the box and inserted her key and had Scott do the same.

"Here you go. I will be right outside. Take your time." The pleasant lady smiled and headed toward the exit of the vault.

"Okay. Thank you." Scott inhaled a deep breath and shifted his eyes to the locker. He pulled out an army-green metal box a little smaller than a shoe box. He unlatched the latches and slowly lifted the lid.

He first noticed a birth certificate along with some other paper work. Scott unfolded the birth certificate and read the name on it. *Shannon Lynn Brimmer;* Father: *Steve Brimmer;* Mother: *Sharon Brimmer* –

Born: *July 16, 1974* Location: *Trinity Hospital in Orange, New York.*

Scott thought for a moment. He didn't recognize the name. He stuffed the paper back in the box and picked up another piece of paper. It was also a birth certificate: *Chandra Ella Gallo* Mother: *Shannon Gallo* Father: *Paul Gallo* Birth: *Hiesler Hospital - New York City, New York, October 8, 1995.*

"Chandy?" Scott said softly. "What the hell is going on?" He pulled out a picture. It was definitely Laura when she was around 14 or 15 years old. She had beautiful long red hair and was wearing blue jeans and a faded tie-dye T-shirt. She was standing in between a middle-aged woman and man. Scott assumed it was her mother and father, but he thought they were killed in a car accident when she was much younger. Could this be her Aunt Lisa? *But she didn't have a husband,* he suddenly recalled.

Scott was getting more and more confused. He flipped over the picture and read the scribbling on the back. *Sharon and Steve Brimmer with Shannon Brimmer 1989.*

"Shannon?" He glanced around the vault to make sure no one else was in there. He held the picture up closer. There was no doubt in his mind that it was Laura. *But was Laura really Shannon? Why would she change her identity? Was Bruce Hoover that bad of a man? Was Laura Peck really a deceased woman? And is Shannon still alive? Is this all a plot to let us know?* Scott's head was rattling with puzzling questions. His adrenaline increased with the thought of Laura...*Shannon* being alive but quickly lessened as he realized the danger she must be in if she had to go into hiding. He tucked all the paperwork into his briefcase and grabbed the stack of pictures.

He got out his notebook and quickly scribbled a note.

*If you are alive, I will find you. I love you Laura! I am not mad. If your true identity is Shannon Brimmer or Shannon Gallo, I'm sure you had a good reason for not telling me. I will protect Chandy always. And we will find you. I promise you.*

*Love and miss you so much,*
*Scott*

Scott hadn't realized he was crying until a tear slid down his cheek and hit the floor. He used the back of one hand to wipe the tears and quickly shoved the note into the metal box with the other. He stuck the green box back into the safe.

Scott motioned to the lady outside the door that he was done, and she escorted him out toward the front of the bank.

He couldn't wait to call Chandy. She'd be thrilled when he told her what all he had found. He couldn't believe this was happening so fast. He suddenly felt guilty for not believing Chandy when she'd tried to tell him that her mom had been leaving her clues.

Scott quickly flagged down the nearest taxi. He was anxious to dive into the paperwork and try to figure out what it all meant. He decided he'd wait until he was back in the room to call Chandy. He glanced at his watch; it was still set to central time. It would be another hour before school would be out anyway. He thought he'd grabbed something from the lobby to take back to the room to eat for lunch. He didn't want to waste any time. *He had a wife to find!* And he'd been waiting long enough. He paid the taxi driver and hurried toward the entrance of the hotel. He glanced up toward the sky and said silently, *so help me, God, if anyone has hurt her, I will kill them!*

\*\*\*

Chandy was thrilled when the last bell of the day rang. It didn't take her anytime to throw her books into her locker and hurry out to Kyle's car. She'd even beat him there which she seldom done.

"Hey, what's your hurry, you missed me that much?" Kyle teased as he approached his car.

Chandy smiled. "Ha ha smart butt. Come on, let's go." She hurriedly slid into the passenger's seat.

"Okay, okay."

"Sorry, but dad is supposed to call me. I kind of wanted to be at home when he did."

"Oh," Kyle glanced at Chandy with raised eyebrows. "You don't want me to be around?"

"It's not that." She didn't know quite how to explain it to him.

"It's okay. I need to run by Doug's anyway. He wanted me to go to the gym with him."

"Thanks for understanding."

"I didn't say I understood," he said in a serious tone. He suddenly laughed, "Gotcha!"

Chandy giggled. "You're not right."

"What time you want me back?" He winked. "Remember I'm babysitting you. Your dad is counting on me."

She grinned. "You don't have to, but if you are brave and willing, I could show you how good of a cook I am."

"You're on! If I can eat your cooking, I am capable of doing almost anything, right?"

Chandy giggled. He always had a way of putting her in a good mood.

They exchanged stories on their events at school as he drove the rest of the way.

Kyle slowly pulled up in front of her house and shifted the Mustang into park. His face grew serious as he leaned over to kiss her. "You know I'm just having fun with you, don't you? I really do care what you find out about your mom today."

"I know you do." She returned his kiss and jumped out of the car. "Call me later."

"I will. Good luck."

"Thanks." She ran into the house and flipped the new alarm off. She let the dogs out and checked her phone again to make sure she hadn't missed any calls. After fixing a glass of tea, and letting Ginger and Zita back in, she settled in front of the TV and patiently waited for her cell phone to ring.

She didn't have to wait long. Chandy's ring tone sung out, and she snatched her cell phone. Her heart raced—it was her dad. "Hi, Dad! Please tell me you have good news!"

"I do. Grab a pen and paper. And you better sit down."

Chandy snatched up the pen and paper on the end table. "I got it. I'm ready." She was so excited, she thought she'd burst! "Hurry, Dad!"

Scott laughed. "Okay, okay. First, I want to apologize for not believing you before, because now I do believe your mother may be alive."

Chandy's heart raced. She jumped to her feet and screamed, "Omigod! I told you! What was it? What did you find?"

"I think I found your mother's original birth certificate and a social security card. I think you were right about her taking Laura Peck's identity, although I don't know why yet."

"I knew it! What is mom's real name?" She didn't know why that was so important to her right now. But for some reason she felt like this information is what her mom had been trying to tell her. *But why*, she wondered.

"I think it is Shannon Lynn Brimmer and she was born in Orange, New York.

"That name is so pretty." She scribbled the name down and asked her dad to spell the last name for her. "What else was in the box?"

Her father hesitated. "Umm…just some pictures and a few other documents."

"What kind of pictures and documents?" She sensed the hesitation in her dad's voice. It almost seemed like he was withholding something. But she couldn't imagine why her dad would hold out any information that would help find her mom.

"Just pictures of your mom with her mother and father and some addresses and bank statements and stuff like that. I haven't examined everything closely yet."

"Are you sure it's mom in the pictures?"

"Yes, I'm positive."

"So, if there's no doubt that it is her on the birth certificate," She drummed the pen on the notebook. "What now?"

"Well, I found out Orange is only about an hour from here. I think I'm going to go down and see if I can find her mom and dad if they are still living. She had said they were killed in a car accident, but that was actually Laura Peck's parents. So maybe her parents are still living. If they are, they probably don't even know she is missing."

"Maybe they don't even know she moved to Missouri. Maybe mom had a falling out with them and she just didn't want us to know about it." She paused. "Darn it! I wish I was with you!" Chandy was furious she hadn't gone with her dad. She should have just missed school. This was far more important.

"Don't worry, Chan, I will call you as soon as I know something."

"I know. I just wish I was there."

"I know you do baby girl, but I'll find the answers we are looking for. Is Kyle with you?"

"Not yet. I wanted to be alone when I talked to you. He's going to the gym and then he will be over."

"Oh, okay." There was a brief silence and then Scott continued, "Is the alarm on?"

"Shoot, I forgot to turn it back on when I let the dogs in. I'm going to run out and grab the mail. I promise I will turn it on as soon as I get back to the house. And I won't go out the rest of the night!" She didn't mind her dad being so overprotective. He'd been like that for the last three years—ever since her mom had disappeared. "Will that you make happy?"

"It would. Thank you, Chan. I just worry about you. You're my life, you know."

"I know you do, Dad. Now get going. You'll be running out of daylight."

"Okay, I will talk to you after a while. Love you, baby girl."

"Love you too. Call me as soon as you know something. Bye."

"Bye." Scott quickly added, "Don't forget the alarm."

Chandy laughed. "I won't, I promise. Bye Dad." She placed her cell phone on the end table. "Omigod, momma's alive. I knew it! I knew it!" She couldn't help but jump up and down. She started singing loudly. "Mamma's alive! Oh yeah she is!" She didn't think she'd ever been this happy. The dogs suddenly started barking. Chandy laughed, "What? You don't like my singing?" She took her glass to the kitchen. *Whoops, the alarm,* she thought. "I'm going now to get the mail, father dear, and I promise I will turn the alarm on when I come back in," she said out loud to no one. "So, you can stop worrying about me!" She shouted, "Just bring my momma home to me!" She stepped outdoors. Nothing could ruin this day.

*So, she thought.*

CHAPTER FOURTEEN

Her heart had skipped a beat when she'd seen Scott leaving with a suitcase. She felt sick of her stomach for what she had done to him. But she hadn't had a choice.

She'd parked at her usual spot before the sun ever came up. She'd wanted to beat Micky in case Chandy decided to go to school early again.

But she hadn't expected Scott to walk out first *and with a suitcase*. She knew that could only mean one thing, a business trip. It wasn't unusual—*just extremely bad timing*. He sometimes had to fly to different areas of the country for meetings or training. She knew it was part of his job.

She stayed at the same spot most of day only leaving long enough to grab a bite to eat. She wanted to make sure Mick didn't tamper with anything around the house while Scott was gone. She wasn't sure what he was up to, but she didn't trust him one bit—especially if Paul was behind the callous plot.

She'd seen Chandy get in Kyle's car and go to school at the usual time. Kyle dropped her back off right after school.

She yawned and unzipped her jacked. She climbed off the bike and strolled toward the top of the hill to see if Micky was still parked in the same spot that he usually was. "Shit!" she mumbled. She quickly scanned the area. He wasn't anywhere near there. Her eyes traveled back to the house, but Micky's car wasn't there either. She scanned the country roads, looking for any sight of the black Cadillac, but it was nowhere to be seen.

At least, Chandy was safe inside the house, but where was the damn prick.

"Damn it!" Her mind raced. She knew any kind of change in Micky's routine wasn't a good sign.

*What should I do?* She was terrified of what Micky's plans were. Her hands trembled as she stuffed them in her pockets. She wasn't sure why she was shaking so much. She wasn't sure if it was her nerves or the cold, or a combination of both.

She couldn't think straight but there was no way she could go to Chandy...not yet. *It's not in the plan*, she thought*, but none of this was!* A few tears escaped, and she flicked them off with the back of her hand. Now wasn't the time for her to be weak. She climbed on the bike and rested her head on the handle bars.

After a few minutes of silence, she lifted her head. Her mind was made up. She'd just wait. *Maybe he just ran to get something to eat,* she tried to convince herself.

She refused to leave her spot until she knew what Micky was up to. She'd sleep under the stars if she had to *or—not sleep at all*! She had only one goal in life and that was to protect Chandy! That was all she cared about.

***

The taxi pulled down the block of Benton Street in Orange, New York. Scott had taken a bus to Orange and then grabbed a taxi to take him to 925 Benton Street. It was the address he'd located in the phone book where Sharon and Steve Brimmer lived. The driver stopped at a small single-story house at the end of the block. The numbers on the mailbox read 925. Scott asked the cab driver if he would stick around and drive him back to the bus station. The driver agreed and pulled out a magazine to read.

Scott climbed out of the taxi and glanced up and down the street. It was a rundown neighborhood; the houses were old and in need of repairs. Some of them were vacant and had 'For Sale' signs in the un-mowed yards. A few kids were playing kick ball in the front lawn of the house next door. He hesitated as he stared up at the dirty beige house. Scott glanced toward the windows; the curtains were drawn. He noticed they were faded and outdated. The house was definitely in need of a paint job; it was chipping away in many places and the worn wood could be seen.

Scott hadn't a clue what he going to say to these people. He hadn't even thought about that part. He clutched his briefcase tightly. Suddenly, he was nervous. He'd never been this uneasy while visiting clients. He was used to going to houses even in the

116

worst neighborhoods. But this was different. This was happening so fast it was almost as if he was in a dream moving in slow motion. His worse fear was that he would wake up any moment and realize it was all a dream. And Laura was still missing and presumably, more than likely, dead.

Scott shook the thought and walked up the crazed sidewalk. He stopped in front of the aged screen door and took a deep breath. He knocked lightly and waited. He was certain he'd heard movement. Scott knocked harder and waited. He glanced down at his business suit and imagined if they had peeked out and seen him, he probably scared them. He looked more like an IRS employee making a house call.

Suddenly he heard a faint, weak female voice from the other side of the door. "Yes, what do you want? I'm not interested in vacuums or anything else you are selling!"

Of course, she would think that, Scott thought amusingly. "I promise I am not selling anything. I am here to talk to you about your daughter. Are you Laura...I mean Shannon Brimmer's mother?"

Silence on the other side.

Scott waited and just when he thought she wasn't going to open the door, it opened slightly, and she peaked through.

He had his insurance card ready and opened the screen door and shoved it through the crack. "I am Scott Hayes. I am married to your daughter."

She was quick to respond. "That is impossible." She opened the door more. "Shannon is married to Paul Gallo."

Scott recognized the last name from the birth certificate *Chandra Gallo.* "I would like to talk to you and your husband about your daughter."

The petite lady opened the door all the way and motioned for him to enter. "That's impossible too. My husband is dead. He died a couple of years ago." She led him into the living room and pointed to a worn-out recliner. "He was a heavy drinker—and it finally destroyed his liver."

Scott quickly dropped into the recliner while wondering if Laura knew about her father. He stared curiously at the elderly lady. It looked like at one time she'd had red hair but most of it was gone now, taken over by a silver-gray color. He could defiantly see the resemblance of his wife and her. "I'm so sorry to hear that."

She laughed. "Don't worry about it. I've never been happier."

Scott was caught off guard by her harsh words but was certain she was being sincere. He wasn't quite sure how to respond, so he decided to change the subject. "When was the last time you saw your daughter?"

Her demeanor quickly changed, and her eyes clouded over. "It's been many years."

"Why?" He couldn't help his sudden question. Scott couldn't imagine why any mother would go years without seeing her daughter.

"It's complicated story." She tried to smile. "Are you really her husband now?"

"I am, but I know her as Laura not Shannon."

She looked puzzled. "Why?"

"I'm not sure. I am trying to figure this out. See your daughter went missing over three years ago and hasn't been seen since. Just lately she has been leaving her daughter and me clues that she is alive." He shook his head. "I am just looking for anything that might help me find her. But first I need to know why she changed her identity?"

Her eyes widen. "Her daughter? I have a grandchild?"

Scott couldn't help but pity the woman. Why hadn't Laura shared the news of Chandy with her own mom? She seemed to be a nice lady and extremely lonely. She didn't seem to be the type that could be violent. He was puzzled. "You didn't know that she'd given birth?"

She hesitated. "I wasn't allowed to have contact with her." Sharon stood and crossed the room to a box of tissues. She snatched one and blew her nose. "It has been so many years, but I have always regretted what we did to Shannon." A few tears escaped down her cheek before she caught them with the tissue. "I couldn't do anything about it though. I had no say in anything back in those days."

Scott was on the edge of the chair now. He was scared to speak in case he spoke the wrong words. He was afraid she would decide not to share any more with him.

She strolled toward the front window and stared out. "It was Steve's fault. His damn whiskey and gambling ruined all of our lives!"

Scott continued to remain silent. His curiosity was increasing by the second. *What the hell happened to Laura,* he wondered.

"Steve had gotten us in a huge financial mess and decided to gamble to get us out of debt." She paced in front of the window. "Well, his planned backfired and he ended up having to borrow money from a powerful mafia man known as Gino Gallo. For a while we were able to keep our house, and we had food on the table again." She looked up toward the sky. "Steve slowed down on his drinking and he quit gambling." She shook her head. "So, we thought. He'd started again— without my knowledge. And Gino was on to him continuously about the money he owed him. It became a bad situation, so bad that we feared that he would kill my husband." Sharon moved over the couch and sat down across from Scott. "Sometimes, I wish he would have!"

Scott was certain the woman meant every word.

"Anyway, we were having dinner one night just me and Shannon and her brother Shawn. Their father was out again on one of his drunken adventures. I heard the knock on the door and there was no doubt in my mind that it was Gino Gallo himself after his money."

Scott stared at the woman intensely. He could tell she was a million miles away as if she was living the nightmare all over again.

"I opened the door and in walked Gino and his son, Paul Gallo. They left me threatening messages to give Steve. They didn't seem to care that Shawn and Shannon were sitting at the table, listening to the whole conversation." She paused, and her voice grew heavy. "I saw the way Paul had been looking at Shannon and it was disturbing. But it was even more disturbing when my husband came home one night and told me that he'd worked out a deal with Gino. He'd said we no longer owed him any money." Her eyes met Scott's. "I knew there was no way Gino was going to let us off that easy. I knew better. He was a ruthless man!" She nodded. "And I was right. Steven had agreed to an arranged marriage for Shannon to Paul Gallo in return to let us out of our debt."

Scott was shocked. "Are you serious?"

Her eyes seemed to be pleading with Scott to believe her. She continued, "I couldn't do anything about it. It was out of my hands. I had no choice!"

"You sold your daughter off?"

Sharon wiped at the tears. "I know it sounds horrible, and I wish I could take it all back." She hesitated.

Scott knew she was reliving the nightmare all over again.

She continued, "Shannon ran away from Paul about a year after they were married. I will never forget the look on her face when I turned her away and called Paul to come and get her." She could no longer control the tears streaming down her face. "I had to, though. He would have killed us all."

"Wow," Scott said. He was stunned, and his heart was breaking for his lost wife. What a horrible life she'd been dealt. It seemed so unfair. And to have your own parents throw you under the bus like that. He shook his head in disbelief. "I don't know what to say."

"If I could do it all over again, I would have taken Shannon and Shawn and left my husband. I would have moved far away and got me a job." She inhaled a deep breath. "But no, I was such a fool. I sold my daughter off to the mafia and my son ended up in prison for robbery. I guess I'm not any trophy mom."

Scott wasn't about to offer this woman sympathy. As far as he was concerned she got what she deserved, and he was glad she was all alone now—served her right for what she'd done. He stood and walked to the door. He didn't feel like sharing anything more about Laura with this woman. He just wanted to be alone and away from this appalling woman.

"If you find her, will you tell her I love her and that I'm sorry." She followed Scott outside. "I really am sorry. I would love to meet my granddaughter."

Even though Scott had no desire to ever contact this woman again, he thought there might be some more information he might need from her one day, so he shouldn't be rude to her just in case. "I will tell her. Thank you so much for your help today."

She followed him out to the cab, rambling non-stop on how it wasn't her fault.

Scott nodded and climbed into the taxi. "Have a good day. Thank you, again." He pulled the door shut.

He motioned to the driver that he was ready. That was one woman he hoped he never had to see again! There was no excuse for what they had done to his wife. He leaned his back against the seat and closed his eyes. *My poor Laura...I love and miss you so much!*

## CHAPTER FIFTEEN

Chandy whistled *'As the Saints Go Marching In'* as she walked down the long, curvy driveway to their mailbox. The dogs were barking like crazy inside the house. They had wanted to come with her, but Ginger had a mind of her own. Chandy knew that if she'd let them go, Ginger would have wandered into the woods like she always does, and she'd end up spending the entire evening trying to find her.

She couldn't quit thinking about her dad's words and everything he had said about her mother. *Shannon Brimmer*, she thought silently. *What was her mother's big secret,* she wondered for the hundredth time.

She reached the end of the driveway and crossed the road over to their mailbox. She flipped open the box and pulled out a handful of letters. As she thumbed through the bills, she heard a nearby car approaching. She didn't immediately look up because she assumed it was Kyle. Chandy finally glanced up just as the car reached her. She gasped and jumped backwards as the black car nearly ran her off the road. She about died when she realized it was the same dreaded black Cadillac.

Suddenly, fear engulfed her. She glanced up the drive toward the house and immediately regretted not letting Ginger and Zita go with her. She knew she didn't have time to run back up the driveway.

Before she even realized what was happening the driver of the Cadillac had slammed on the brakes and the creepy peeping-tom guy jumped out of the car. He was wearing a long black trench coat and a dark stocking cap. Chandy screamed as the guy grabbed her around the waist and pulled her toward the car.

She screamed for Ginger and Zita, not knowing who else to scream for. She knew she was wasting her breath; there wasn't any way the dogs could get out of the house and there were no other houses nearby.

Chandy kicked and screamed with everything she had, but the guy overpowered her. He held her tightly with one hand while quickly lifting the trunk of the car with the other. *Omigod,* she thought as she realized what his intentions were. She bent her head forward and bit his arm as hard as she could.

"Ouch! You fucking bitch!" He smacked her across the face and shoved her into the trunk. He pulled her flying arms together and tied them together with rope. He next grabbed her kicking feet and applied pressure while bounding them together.

"Please don't hurt me," Chandy cried. "I will give you anything you want. I have lots of money at the house." Although she was lying, she thought if she could get him back to the house her dogs would attack him while she activated the alarm.

Chandy had never been so scared in her life. She was certain he planned on raping her and killing her. She'd heard about these sorts of things happening all the time. She just never dreamed it could happen to her.

"Shut up." He grabbed a rag and crammed it into her mouth.

She tried to spit it out, but he had lodged it in securely.

Suddenly she froze, she heard something coming down the road. It sounded like a motorcycle. *Hurry, hurry, help me,* she prayed. She hoped someone would witness her in the trunk and call the police.

But it was too late. The guy had heard the oncoming motor vehicle too. He hurriedly slammed the trunk closed. Chandy listened as he jumped into the driver's seat and slammed the car into drive.

Her heart sunk as the tears flowed. No one would ever find her now. She sobbed uncontrollably and wondered what her destiny was. *How could this be happening now?* She was so close to finding her mom! She thought of her dad and how sad he would be. She knew Kyle would be returning to the house at any time now. She was certain he'd call the police when she couldn't be found. *But how would they ever find her?* Her sobs increased as she realized she'd never told her dad about the black Cadillac being the same peeping Tom. He wouldn't have a clue where to start looking for her. *By the time they find me, I'd probably be dead anyway,* she thought. *How could I have been so stupid and naïve?* Her dad had warned her to be careful and she'd let her guard down. Now, she might not ever see her mom again! With that thought she twisted and fought to get out of the bondage. She refused to become the next victim to this pervert. She would fight like hell to get away from this creep or die trying.

*** 

She hadn't seen it coming but had witnessed the whole scene. She was up on the hill when she saw Chandy coming out of the house and heading down the driveway.  At first, she cursed at her silently for leaving the house alone, but as soon as she noticed that Micky still hadn't returned to his usual spot, she let out of sigh of relief.

She'd assume Chandy was just going down to the mailbox and she was right. She breathed a little easier as Chandy crossed the street to the mailbox, but as she watched her pulling the letters out of the box, she suddenly heard a familiar sound. She glanced down the road and saw Micky's black Cadillac coming toward Chandy.

"Omigod! Run Chandy," she screamed.

She watched in horror as Micky jumped out of the car and grabbed Chandy.

She threw down the half-eaten candy bar and snatched up her helmet. She flung it on her head without fastening it and fired up the motorcycle. Her heart was beating faster than ever. She shifted the bike in gear and peeled out after the car.

But unfortunately, he must have heard the motorcycle.  As she approached the top of the hill, she saw Micky looking back her way. He'd hurriedly jumped in the car and sped away. She rode faster than she ever had before, trying to catch up with him. But it was useless. She lost him.

She drove the long way back to highway B, but they were nowhere in sight.

She stopped at the stop sign and looked both ways. She didn't have a clue which way to go. "Damn it!" She beat the handle bars with her fist. "Why, now?" she screamed into the air. The tears surfaced. All the planning, all the sacrifices she'd made to save her daughter from this God-awful man was for nothing now! *Paul, you fuck bastard! You finally won,* she thought silently.

Now, he would have their daughter and she'd marry into the mafia and her life would be hell the way hers had been. Laura shook her head in defeat. She knew she could go to jail for all the lies she'd disclosed over the years and her bogus disappearance. And she had illegally taken Chandy away from her father. She bit her lip and fought back the uncontrollable tears. *And Scott*—he would never forgive her for all that she had done to him. The only thing that probably kept him going was Chandy and now she was gone also!

She drove toward the motel. Her only hope was that he was taking Chandy back there. But she was sure that was highly unlikely. He'd probably already been ordered to check out of the motel and snatch Chandy while Scott was away.

She knew she couldn't go to the police. Maybe she should call Scott, or maybe she should go back and wait for Kyle and then have him call the police. But she was sure they would take her in for questioning and her daughter would be long gone by the time she was released *if she was even released.*

Once again, she allowed herself to think of her mom and dad. "This is all your fault," she mumbled. She'd never understood how her own parents could sell their own child the way they did. And it would be cold day in hell before she ever forgave them.

Just like she assumed, she pulled up to the motel and there was no black Cadillac anywhere on the property.

The tears increased as she hurried into her own room and gathered the few things she'd left. Her mind was wrestling with the choices that she had.

She blew her nose and cleared her throat. She placed the room key on the TV and scanned the room to make sure she hadn't left any clues. Her mind was made up. She had only one goal in life and that was to save Chandy. What happens to herself didn't matter anymore. *Who could save Chandy better than herself? And who knew more about the situation than herself?*

She knew where Chandy was going. There was no doubt that Paul would have Micky bring her to him in New York.

She fastened her helmet and buttoned her coat up. She had a long drive ahead of her. She was going to New York on her bike. It would be at least a two-day journey, but she imagined that was how Chandy would get there too. Micky wouldn't risk putting her on an airplane.

*I am so sorry, Chandy. You don't deserve this. I failed you in every way,* she thought. *Don't worry, sweetie, I'm going to find you and take care of this for once and for all. I should have done this a long time ago.* She knew exactly what she had to do!

***

It was after 9:00 p.m. when Scott told his buddies goodnight. He rubbed his forehead as he waited for the elevator. The mixture of coke and rum, and the loud rock and roll band had set on a headache. He pulled his phone out of his pocket. He hadn't checked it for the last couple of hours and was surprised he hadn't heard from Chandy.

He was shocked to see he had seven missed calls from Chandy and five calls from an unknown number. "Wow," he mumbled as he climbed on the elevator. He couldn't believe he hadn't heard his phone going off even once. He didn't take time to check his voice messages. Instead, he quickly called Chandy.

Scott was surprised to hear Kyle's voice instead of Chandy's.

"Oh, thank God, Scott, is that you?"

Scott knew instantly something wasn't right. "Kyle? Is something wrong? Is Chandy alright?"

Kyle's voice was frantic. "She's not here. I'm at your house now. I went to the gym and got here about six and she was gone."

Scott was baffled. "What do you mean she wasn't there? Where is she?"

Kyle rambled on, "Her phone is here with her purse. The front door was unlocked, and Zita and Ginger were barking like crazy. I've looked everywhere in the house. I've been all over the grounds. I found some of your letters scattered by the mailbox, so I checked out in the woods too. I yelled for her and everything."

"Are you kidding? Omigod!" He entered the hotel room, dropping the keys on the bed.

Kyle's voice quivered, "She told me to go to the gym. I shouldn't have left her."

Suddenly, the night of Laura's disappearance flashed before Scott's eyes. He couldn't go through that again. "Have you called the police yet?"

"I did but they wouldn't let me file a missing report until 24 hours are up."

"Of course, they probably think she ran away without her phone or purse!" He rolled his eyes. "Why can't the police just use common sense and realize she's not a runaway!" Kyle didn't reply. "I'm sorry, Kyle. Don't blame yourself for this. We will find her."

"I'm so sorry, Scott. I have never loved a girl before like your daughter."

Scott could tell he'd struggled with the words. He was all choked up. "I'm going to check my voice mails and then call and schedule a flight back there as soon as I can."

"I just wanted you to know how much I care about her," Kyle continued as if Scott hadn't even spoken. "I don't think I can live without her."

"Kyle, listen to me. Get a hold of yourself. I am going to need your help if we plan on finding her. You need to be strong for Chandy."

"I know. I'm sorry. I'm just so shook up over this. I'm really worried."

"I know you are. So am I," Scott agreed.

"What if she is hurt somewhere?" Kyle asked.

"Did you check the basement and make sure she didn't fall down the stairs doing laundry or something?" Scott suddenly had a horrible image of Chandy lying at the bottom of the stairs covered with blood.

"Yes, I already look down there. I tell you I have been all over this house. At first I thought she was just playing with me and hiding from me." He paused. "But that was wishful thinking."

Scott suddenly had a bizzare thought. Maybe Laura came back for her. Oh God, that would be the only solution he'd accept. But he couldn't imagine Laura doing it that way—without telling him first. She knew he would be devastated. Surely, she wouldn't do that twice to him. "Hey, Kyle, stay put just in case she comes back. Turn the alarm on though."

"I'm not going anywhere. I've already fed the dogs and let them out. I'm waiting for her right here."

"Have you called any of her friends? Why don't you go through her phone and call her friends to see if any of them have seen her? I am going to make a few calls myself and I will call you back. Call me if you hear anything."

"I promise, I will."

"Put my number in your cell phone too," Scott added.

"Okay, I will. Talk to you soon."

He glanced at the time while he dialed his voice mail. It was 9:15 p.m. which meant it was 8:15 p.m. back home. The first voice message startled him so much he dropped the phone. He quickly recovered it and replayed the message. It was *her*. There was no

131

doubt that the voice on the other end was *his Laura*. And she knew about Chandy.

He listened for the third time.

*Scott, I'm sorry for all the pain I have caused you. I hope you will understand one day why I did what I did. But I need your help more than ever now. You must help me save Chandy. I am not sure where you are at, but I need you to meet me in New York. I know who has Chandy and I know they are headed to New York. I don't think they will hurt her. I will explain later. I should be there in a couple of days and will get in contact with you then for further instructions. I understand if you would rather go to the police, but I really hope you wait until you hear me out. I did this all for Chandy....*

Her voice faded away, and all he could think about was that *Laura was alive*. He fell to his knees and bowed his head on the bed and cried like he'd never cried before.

## CHAPTER SIXTEEN

After several endless hours, Chandy gave up trying to escape from the tightly bound ropes around her legs and hands. It was useless. She was so exhausted. She didn't know how long she'd been in the trunk, but it seemed like they had been driving forever. She couldn't imagine where he was taking her. She figured if all he wanted was to have his way with her, he would have already done so. She considered he'd kidnapped her for ransom, but quickly dismissed that theory. Her dad didn't have a lot of money. Although she was certain he would get it if he had to.

She knew Kyle would have called the police by now. Maybe they would find her soon. She fought to stay awake, but she was so tired from struggling. Maybe she should sleep so she would have strength to fight off her abductor if she got the chance. Finally, she dozed off.

She didn't know how long she'd been asleep when she felt the car come to a sudden halt. It took her a few minutes to realize that she was still in a trunk of a car and none of this was another one of her nightmares like she had hoped it to be.

She heard him get out of the car and slam the door shut. She was certain he was coming back to get her. *Omigod,* she thought. *This is it. He is going to rape and kill me now.*

After several minutes had passed he lifted the trunk slightly and peeked in. He then continued to open it up all the way. He glared at her. "Okay, listen up, little lady, you do as I say, and I won't need to use this." He pulled a revolver from the back of his jeans and pointed it at her. "You make one wrong move or try to escape, and I won't hesitate to blow that pretty little head off that sexy body of yours." His eyes narrowed. "Do you understand?"

Chandy nodded and hoped the lunatic didn't see how bad she was trembling. She was sure that this creep meant everything he said. And she didn't have any intention of dying from the hands of this maniac if she could help it.

He untied the rope around her legs and arms and pulled the gag out of her mouth. "Get out!" he demanded.

Chandy was somewhat dizzy but managed to climb out of the trunk. She glanced around at her surroundings, trying to take it all in. It was dark out, but she could tell they were on some kind of gravel road. There were trees in every direction. She didn't see a house or a road sign anywhere.

"Go relieve yourself and don't try anything funny."

She was kind of shocked when he handed her a few paper towels. *You mean I don't have to drip-dry? You're way too kind,* she wanted to shout, but didn't dare.

She went to the front of the car and squatted. This might be her only chance to escape. She could run through the woods. Chandy quickly dismissed the thought, she knew he could easily catch her, and she was certain he would shoot her for sure. *No this wasn't the time. Not yet,* she thought.

After she finished she returned to the back of the car. He handed her a sandwich and a bottle of water. "Eat!"

"Where are you taking me?" She instantly regretted her probing question as he back handed her across the face. She jumped and nearly dropped her sandwich.

"Did I say you could talk?" he growled.

She shook her head as the throb in her cheek lingered. She decided she wouldn't say another word—no matter what. She wasn't going to do anything else to upset this livid man. She'd just witnessed the fuming rage in his eyes, and she knew he wouldn't hesitate to kill her. She was going to do everything in her power not to upset this nut. She feared for her life. And every moment she could stay alive would be a moment closer to getting rescued.

She ate her sandwich and drank the water in silence. The guy pointed the gun to the inside of the trunk. "Get in."

She quickly climbed in and was surprised that he didn't even bother to bind her legs and arms. He didn't put the gag back in her mouth either, and she was thankful—she could breathe easier. He slammed the trunk down, and she heard him climbing in the car.

She laid in terror for several moments while waiting for the car to start up. When it didn't—she thought he'd changed his mind and was coming back for her. This time he would kill her she was sure of it.

She laid awake for a bit—waiting. But she was so tired, and her head was pounding. She felt strangely odd almost as if she was half-way drunk. Her eyes fluttered shut. She couldn't stay awake any longer. She drifted off to sleep, dreaming of her horrible destiny.

*\*\*\**

Scott hadn't slept much through the night. His head was full of unanswered questions. He'd spent most of the night going through Laura's metal box again and again, trying to piece the puzzle together. He wondered what Laura knew about Chandy's whereabouts and how she knew. *And why had she left her own daughter and the man that loved her more than anyone?* He didn't get it, but he would forgive her for any reason she had because he loved her more than life itself.

He had called Kyle before going to bed and asked him not to call the police yet. Kyle had been surprised at Scott's request.

Scott tried to explain that he might know where Chandy was headed, but he was careful not to give any details about Chandy's mother being alive. He told Kyle that he really couldn't talk about it, but once they got Chandy back, he would explain everything. Scott told him that she might be with a family member heading to New York where she was born. He asked Kyle not to say anything to anyone just yet.

Kyle accepted his statement and seemed relieved to hear that Chandy might be alright. He agreed to stay at the house until Scott got back just in case Chandy did return.

Scott trusted Kyle and believed that he would keep quiet. And he was glad that he was staying at the house and didn't have to worry about finding someone to take care of Zita and Ginger. Chandy was lucky to have such a good kid as a boyfriend.

Although he was still worried like hell about Chandy, Laura's voice mail almost reassured him that she would be okay. He had to believe it. Although he couldn't even image what Chandy was going through or how scared she must be.

He thought of the peeping Tom from the other night and wondered if he had something to do with all of this. He pulled out his the lighter that Bobby had found behind the house: *Gallo BBQ*. He stared curiously at the lighter. He knew there had to be a connection and then it suddenly hit him. *Gallo— Chandra Gallo—Gallo BBQ. Chandy's real father? Was he the peeping-tom?*

Suddenly, he was hungry for BBQ. *Is that who has Chandy?* Scott was certain he was on to something. Maybe he wouldn't have to wait for Laura to explain it all to him.

He hurried to shower and got dressed. He planned on showing up to the meeting at nine just, so no one expected anything unusual. He would sneak out of there early and hit the BBQ place for lunch. And if Paul

Gallo *was* at the joint that would mean he didn't have Chandy.

Scott grabbed his brief case and hurried out of the room. He was certain this was going to be the longest meeting ever. He checked his phone as he entered the elevator. He turned it all the way up. He didn't want to miss any more calls from Laura.

***

Laura drove all night and most of the morning before she got tired. She'd taken several breaks along the way. It had been a cold, long ride and she needed rest.

She'd planned on driving straight to New York, but it was an eighteen-hour drive, and she hadn't realized how tiring it could be on a motorcycle. She knew she needed rest if she planned on saving Chandy.

She pulled off at the next exit and found a Super 8 Motel. After checking into the room, she took a quick shower. She set her alarm for 3:00 p.m. That would give her a little over three hours of sleep and she had about six more hours of driving to do. She thought of Chandy and wondered if Micky was driving straight through. The thought of her daughter in the trunk of that car the whole ride made her sick. But then she thought of the other options, up front with *Mick the Prick*. "Omigod, if you try anything with her Mr. Prick, I will cut it off, so help me," she mumbled out loud. She couldn't let her mind wander down that road or she wouldn't be able to sleep. She couldn't allow herself to freak out, or she would force herself to keep driving and that could end in tragedy if she didn't rest.

She snatched up her cell phone. Laura needed to call Scott and update him. Her hands shook, she was just as nervous as she was when she'd left the voice message for him the night before.

It had to be a total shock for him, getting a voice mail from her. She could only imagine how mad he was for what she has done.

She stared at the phone as she deliberated what she would say to Scott. Her biggest fear was that he would answer. She'd rather leave another voice mail. It was easier that way.

She dialed the number and waited nervously as it rung.

After a couple rings Scott answered, "Laura?"

"Hi Scott."

"Omigod. Is it really you?"

"It is." She hesitated. "I am so sorry for what I have put you through."

There was a long pause. "I don't understand, but I'm sure you had a good reason for what you did. But right now, it doesn't matter. I just want to find our daughter and make sure she is alright."

"I agree. That is why I'm calling. I'm getting ready to sleep for a couple of hours and then I should be up there this evening. Where can we meet?"

"I'm at the Holiday Inn down on Sterling. I am walking into Gallo BBQ as we are speaking."

Laura's heart nearly stopped. "What? What the hell are you doing there?"

"Wow, there're a lot of business men eating here today," he replied.

"Scott, listen to me!" Laura was frantic. "Don't say anything. Just listen to me. Those aren't business men, those are mafia men and they use that place as a cover-up for meetings. Please, don't ask any questions just get a drink or something and get the hell out of there."

There was a long pause and Laura was scared it was already too late. But then she heard him order some BBQ to go. He spoke back into the phone. "Okay, I'm getting some BBQ for our lunch. I will see you a bit, honey." He hung up.

*Omigod!* She didn't know if she could trust Scott to be quiet or not. Once he had his mind made up about something it was hard to convince him otherwise. And he never did scare easily.

She shook her head in disbelief. The situation was slowly turning into a nightmare. Laura let the tears fall as she questioned her plans. Maybe she shouldn't even have told Scott anything at all.

She'd heard many stories that had happened at Gallo's BBQ and right now she feared for Scott's life. She was certain that Paul probably knew that Scott was in New York this weekend and more than likely *he knew what he looked like too!*

.

CHAPTER SEVENTEEN

Scott leaned against the wall as he waited for his order. He sized up the Italian men working behind the counter and the guys eating at the table. He glanced toward the men in the back, playing pool. Scott wondered if any of these guys were Paul Gallo, Chandy's father and Laura's *other* husband. He shivered at the thought of his wife being made to marry one of these men. Although they looked like nice, professional business men, he was certain they were ruthless, hardnosed scoundrels.

He'd heard what Laura had said but if this rat knows anything about where Chandy was, he wasn't going to just stand by and not do anything. He'd been the one to raise Chandy these last three years. She was his daughter, not this low-life crook's, and he wasn't going to back down from anyone—mafia or not!

The big, burly man behind the counter called out, "Number nine, your order is ready."

Scott approached the counter and wondered if the stocky guy was Paul. "Smells great! Do you own this place?"

"No, I just work here." The guy handed Scott the sack of food.

"Oh. Well it is a nice place. Who's the owner?"

The guy's dark eyes narrowed. "Paul Gallo."

"Is he around? I'd like to talk with him."

The dark hair man folded his arms across his chest. "What about?"

Scott held up his briefcase. "I sell insurance just thought I'd see if he needed any of my services."

The guy's eyes remained cold. "He's not here and not interested."

"I see." Scott held up the bag of food. "I really did come for the BBQ just thought I would check while I was here."

The man rolled his eyes and sigh. "Do you have a card? I'll give it to him when he returns?"

*Oh crap,* Scott thought silently. He didn't think he'd ask for that. "I don't—not with me. Maybe I can give him a call later?"

"Or you can just come back later," the guy replied rudely. The husky fellow turned to wait on another customer. He glanced back at Scott. "Sorry, but I got worked to do."

"Sure. I will check back later." Scott kept his head bowed as he exited the joint. He was certain the man behind the counter had been skeptical of him. Maybe he shouldn't have asked but he had to know if that ghastly man was there.

But now he didn't know if the dude had been lying or if Paul really was coming back later. He sighed heavily. He wasn't any closer to finding Chandy.

He needed Paul's address but wasn't sure how he could get it without Laura. Scott was sure she wouldn't give out that information before she got here.

Scott wiped his brow. Patience had never been one of his favorable characteristics. He didn't want to wait for Laura. *What if Paul didn't abduct Chandy? And some pervert had her and was doing God-knows-what to her right now, while we are in New York chasing mafia men? Maybe Laura had it all wrong. How the hell could she know for sure what happened to Chandy?*

The thought of Chandy being hurt in anyway disturbed him. He swatted at a tear. He had to get to his hotel room before he broke down. He didn't know if he could emotionally handle all of this.

He flagged down a taxi and gave the address of the hotel to the driver.

Scott just wanted to get to the room and call Kyle to see if he'd heard anything. Maybe Chandy had been with friends and returned home during the night. He knew that wouldn't be the case but all he could do now is pray for a miracle.

*** 

Chandy stirred awake as she felt the car moving again. She rubbed her eyes as reality set in. Daylight was streaming through the cracks of the trunk. She had no clue how long she'd been asleep or how long they had been driving. Her head ached severely, and she felt dizzy. She tried to recall everything that had happened up until now, but her mind was foggy. She remembered her abductor taking her at the mailbox but everything since then was a blur. She vaguely remembered stopping and the vile man smacking her. Suddenly, she recalled a sandwich and a bottle of water and being so tired. Yes, she was certain the man had drugged her by putting something in the bottle of water. *But why? And where is he taking me now?* She had to be careful from now on about drinking or eating any food that he offered. *But then I'll die of starvation,* she thought. Her eyes filled with tears, it didn't matter either way, she was certain she would die regardless. She thought of her dad—he'd be lost without her. He'd been devastated when her mom had disappeared. She'd hate for him to have to go through that all over again.

She thought of Kyle. She would miss him so much. But she was certain that in time he would get over her and be okay. He would find another girlfriend, and one day he would marry and have a family. She thought about how lucky his wife would be to land such a good man.

She visualized her mother. But this time she didn't visualize her up in heaven waiting for her. Instead she visualized her coming into the house and yelling, *"Chandy, I'm back."*

Chandy didn't try to stop the tears. She knew that would be her luck. So close to finally finding her mom and now she would be tortured and killed, or die of drugs or starvation, and never get to see her mom after all this time waiting.

Her ears suddenly perked at the commotion outside of the car. The noise gradually grew louder. It sounded as if they were in traffic—lots of traffic. She cocked her head and listened. The car suddenly slowed down. She wondered if they were in a traffic jam or maybe they had reached a city. She fiddled with latch on the trunk, trying to get it unlatched. She was certain if the trunk flew open that someone would see her and have to help her or at least call the police.

She hit the latch with her fist. It was useless; she'd never get it unlatched. Maybe she could beat on the trunk. Someone might hear it. After a few moments, she realized that it wasn't such a bright idea after all. Her abductor would probably be the only one to hear it and she was certain he wouldn't be happy about it. She might as well try to stay alive as long as she could. She didn't want to encourage the guy into killing her any faster. She'd just wait it out and pray something hopeful would happen soon. She heard cars honking. She laid her head back down and listened to the chaos surrounding her. She never thought she'd be so happy to hear such noise. She knew that it meant people were nearby and maybe, somehow, she would find a way to escape. All she had was hope, but at least now she had that.

***

It was early evening when Laura reached Scott's hotel. She parked the motorcycle near the back entrance and crawled off slowly. She pulled off her helmet and took a deep breath. It had been a long drive, but now she was more nervous about seeing Scott than anything. She hadn't seen him for over three years and she wasn't sure how he was going to take her sudden exit. Especially, now that he knew it was purposely planned. She hoped he would understand but she couldn't blame him if he didn't. She owed him an explanation for what she had done, and she could only hope for the best. By the outcome of everything, she was certain she'd made all the wrong decisions.

She ran her hand over her fly-away hair and glanced in the mirror on her bike. She was shocked to see the reflection staring back at her. She really hadn't cared how she looked for so long that she didn't realize how much she had changed. She looked as if she'd aged ten years rather than three. Her hair was dyed dark now and chopped off by her own hands. Her skin was darker than usual and looked rough from all the sun and wind while riding the bike. She knew she wasn't the young, attractive redhead that Scott had fallen in love with. Maybe it was best if he wasn't attracted to her any more. It might make all this easier for him. She did love him but still hadn't been convinced that sharing her past would have been the right thing to do. Now, she wished she would have. She was certain he would have stuck by her side and helped her. But it was too late now. It was all water under the bridge and she couldn't change it.

***

Scott tossed his cell phone on the bed and slammed his fist on the desk. "Damn it," he said out loud.

Kyle had no new news for him about Chandy. He kind of assumed that but was just hoping for some kind of a miracle. He rubbed his temples and wondered what his next step should be. He couldn't quit thinking about Paul Gallo, *Chandy's real father.* It all just blew his mind. It was hard to believe—all that he had learned. He'd give anything if this whole thing was just a terrible nightmare. He'd love to wake up in his own bed and find Chandy sound asleep in her own room. He shook his head. This wasn't the way he wanted Chandy to find out that he wasn't her biological father. He knew this was real—more real than anything he'd ever experienced in his life.

He took a hot shower and settled down at the computer to research Mafia's in the New York area.

He tired after a few hours and called down for some room service. After eating a light meal, he paced in front of the window, wondering what he would say to Laura when she arrived.  The knock on the door suddenly silenced his thoughts. *Could it be her, already?*

He stood and brushed the loose bread crumbs off his clothes. He rushed to the door and then suddenly hesitated. He felt awkward, like he was meeting a blind date for the first time. Scott inhaled a deep breath and pulled the door open.

He knew at once that it was her. The dark, hacked hair-cut couldn't disguise the beautiful face that he had fallen in love with. For a few moments, neither of them spoke. He had dreamed of this moment since the day she had gone missing. And suddenly emotions overwhelmed him. He pulled her into the room and flung his arms around her petite body. Tears streamed from his eyes and the sobs were uncontrollable. She held him tightly and cried with him.

Scott knew at that moment there wasn't anything in this world that she could say to make him change the way he felt about her. He loved her as much as he did the day she'd disappeared. Reality suddenly set in and he realized why she was here—*Chandy. How could this be the best and the worst day of his life?*

## CHAPTER EIGHTEEN

Chandy listened as the outside noise lessened. It seemed like the further the guy drove the less chaotic it sounded outside. She was just starting to second-guess her earlier decision about beating on the trunk when the vile man slowed down.

She positioned her body, so she could hear better and turned her ear toward the front of the car. The car slowly came to a stop, and he killed the engine.

Chandy held her breath as she waited to see what her next venture would be. She realized he could kill her at any time, but the longer he waited the more she started thinking maybe that wasn't the plan.

He raised the trunk and glared down at her. "Get out!"

She climbed out and tried to adjust her eyes to the daylight. As he slammed the trunk she allowed herself to glance around at her surroundings. She stood in front of a massive, up-scaled house. She looked over her shoulder in the direction they had come. She was surrounded by a huge iron gate. Outside and across the road were more exquisite homes. A dozen or so moving vehicles were visible. There were some people riding bikes and a few couples walking. She felt like she was on the outskirts of a big city.

"Come on." The guyed nodded toward the house.

Chandy glanced toward the gate again, wondering if she could outrun this creep. She figured once she got outside the gate someone would be willing to help her.

The guy interrupted her thought. "Don't even think about it." He pointed to the gun bulging out of his jeans. "I don't have a problem shooting you right here. And the cops here in New York would take about two hours to get here, *if they'd come at all,* and I'll be long gone by then." He shifted his weight to his other foot and rested his hands on his hips. "You're not in Missouri any more, Miss Priss, so move your ass."

His foul tone was enough to scare her into following his instructions. She moved slowly toward the house which was more like a mansion. *New York*, she wondered. *How can they be in New York? Did I really ride in the trunk of a car all the way to New York?* She recalled all the sleeping she had done. No wonder he had drugged her—so she wouldn't give him trouble along the way.

As they approached the front of the house, the big double doors flew open. A petite elderly lady stood drying her hands on her apron. Her skin was a dark tan and Chandy thought she might be Italian.

"Mr. Gallo has been expecting you, Micky." She didn't smile but quickly moved to the side to let them in.

Chandy entered the huge entry way. "Why am I here?" She asked the lady, hoping that she would give her some insight on to what was going on.

The lady ignored her and turned toward the *so-called Micky*. "Mr. Gallo is in the den. You can go on in."

"Thank you, Doris." He glanced toward Chandy; his expression was solemn. "Follow me," he ordered.

Chandy glanced at the striking paintings on the wall as she followed him down the hallway. Most of them were scenic pictures of Italy and Venice. Her mind was full of unanswered questions. It was obvious whoever owned the house had a lot of money. *But what does any of this have to do with me,* she wondered. She wasn't near as scared as she was in the beginning. She was certain if rape or murder were on *Micky's* mind that he would have already done so. Something else was going on and her curiosity was increasing by the moment.

Micky held the door open for Chandy to enter. Suddenly his deposition changed as he shut the door behind him and turned toward the gentleman sitting at the desk. "Hello, sir." He smiled. "I brought you what you requested."

The brawny man didn't speak at first nor did he look up from his computer. He finished whatever he was working on before closing his laptop and pushing it to the side of the desk. He glanced toward Micky, "Thank you, Mick. Now will you please excuse us?"

"Yes, sir."

The man waited until Micky had left the room. His eyes traveled toward Chandy. He didn't speak at first but stared for a few seconds. He reached for a cigar on his desk. "So, what do they call you, now?"

Chandy could feel her hands trembling. "Chandy," she stuttered, "Chandy Hayes." There was something about this man that scared the hell out of her. He had to be well over 6 tall, maybe even 6'5". He was so tall and powerfully built. His hair was thick and dark as night and his eyes matched. She imagined he was Italian and now she understood all the paintings on the walls. She was certain that this was his house. "Who are you?" she whispered. "What do you want from me?"

He puffed on the cigar and slowly blew out the smoke. "I'm not going to beat around the bush." He motioned toward a chair. "You should sit."

Chandy willing dropped down on the sofa leaning against the wall. She crossed her quivering hands in her lap as she waited for him to continue.

"My name is Paul Gallo. I am your father."

Chandra quickly stuttered, "No, you're not. My dad is Scott Hayes. You must have me mixed up with someone else."

He raised his hand to silence her. "Hear me out, young lady."

The sound of his voice was enough to quiet her.

He continued, "As I was saying, my name is Paul Gallo, my wife's name was Shannon Gallo and my daughter's name was Chandra Ella Gallo.

Chandy immediately realized he used his wife's name in the past tense.

He continued, "We had an arranged marriage because that is how we do things in my family." He paced in front of her. His face remained somber. "I was married to your mother, Shannon Gallo and you were born on October 8, 1995. We named you Chandra Ella Gallo." He paused briefly. He seemed to be recalling that day all over again. "Well, your mother got a wild hair to steal you from me." He crushed the cigar in the ashtray as the anger in his voice increased. "I have been trying to find you for the last seventeen years."

Chandy couldn't believe what she was hearing. *It couldn't be possible. Could it?* She just couldn't imagine her mother doing anything of the sort. This just wasn't making sense to her.

"I'm sure you must be in shock." He poured a glass of water from a pitcher and handed it to Chandy. "Believe me, it is the truth." He turned his back on her and walked toward the desk. "I'm sorry for the way Mick had to snatch you. I was scared you wouldn't come if you knew the truth."

Chandy took a few drinks of the water and set it down on the end table. She was overwhelmed and couldn't control the emotion building up any longer. At first it was just a few tears but suddenly they were pouring down her cheeks. "I just want to go home. Please take me home." She snatched a Kleenex from the box on the end table and dabbed at her eyes. "I am sorry for what happened to you and your daughter, but I assure you I'm not the one you are looking for." She blew her nose. "I already have a father. His name is Scott Hayes."

Paul snatched up a photograph lying on the desk and shoved it in Chandy's face. "Does she look familiar?"

Chandy stared blankly at a younger version of her mother, standing next to a younger version of this man. There was no doubt in her mind that it was her mother. She glanced up at the stranger, not wanting this man to be her father, but knowing very well that it was possible now. After seeing the picture of her mom and him together, his story was starting to make sense. *But why mother, would you take me away from my father,* she asked herself silently. She had to believe her mother had a very good reason for what she had done. Maybe this was the *Bruce Hoover* that was so abusive. She closed her eyes. The room was starting to spin. All her mother's lies flashed through her mind. She was so dizzy.

Paul continued to talk about her mother, but Chandy couldn't hear a thing. Her head was killing her. She had to lie down. "I don't feel good." She tried to stand but dizziness took over. She grasped a hold of the couch arm in fear that she would fall.

Suddenly, Doris was beside her and Paul was ordering directions to her. "Take her upstairs and put her to bed. She'll be fine in a few hours."

Chandy didn't recall making it up the stairs or the woman putting her in bed. Her eyes fluttered open briefly as she tried to glance around the room. She was fighting to stay awake, but the bed was so soft, and she wanted to sleep. She was certain she'd been drugged again but she didn't care. And with that last thought she drifted off into a deep sleep.

CHAPTER NINETEEN

Scott sipped on the hot coffee Laura made. He'd forgotten how good she could make coffee. He watched her as she opened the packages of sugar to add to cup.

He couldn't take his eyes off her. Even under the dark chopped hair, she was just as beautiful as the day she disappeared. His intention wasn't to make wild, passionate love to her before they even discussed the situation with Chandy, but he hadn't been able to control himself. He had missed her more than he had realized. He had been convinced that she really was dead. And to see her alive, woke up every emotion inside of him. He never knew he was capable of loving someone so much until now. He hadn't been with another woman since she'd disappeared. He hadn't even considered it. She was the love of his life and if he couldn't have her, he didn't want anyone.

Through tears Laura had told him the same story her mom had told him. It broke his heart to know what she had gone through. And how could her own family disown her like that and sell her like she was property. There were still a lot of things he didn't quite understand but he was sure everything she had done was for a good reason.

Laura lifted her head from her cup. "I know you don't understand why I had to disappear into thin air like I did. And I feel horrible for putting you and Chandy through that. But at the time, I felt like I was doing the right thing."

Scott put his hand over hers. "You don't have to explain anything to me." He touched her cheek. "I love you and I forgive you."

"Please Scott, I need to explain."

Scott's eyes locked with hers. "Okay, if that is what you want, go ahead. But there isn't anything you can say that will change my mind how I feel about you."

"I appreciate that, and I love you too with all my heart." She stood, walked toward the window and gazed out. "I really thought I had thought this through. I had been planning this for years." She turned to look at him. "I had rented a car and had it parked on the other side of the woods the night I vanished." Her eyes watered. "I thought if everyone thought I was dead then Paul would give up on looking for me and Chandy." She wiped away the tears trickling down her cheeks. "I knew if Paul ever found us he would take Chandy, and I would never see her again. He already had an arranged marriage planned for her when she turned eighteen." She crossed the room and grabbed Scott's hands. "I couldn't let that happen. I couldn't let her grow up in the Mafia." She bowed her head and sobbed.

Scott lifted her chin. "Hey, it's okay. I would have done the same thing."

"After a couple years, I started realizing that I had made a bad decision. Although at the time, I thought I was protecting Chandy." She frowned. "I didn't want her to go through life thinking her mother was dead, so I started leaving her hints that I was alive." She dropped Scott's hands and sat back down at the table. She took a sip of coffee and continued, "I decided to change the plan. I wanted her to figure out that I was alive. I assumed after her eightieth birthday had come and gone that Paul would stop looking for us. I knew once she figured out about the safe box at the bank that she would figure the rest out. But..." she hesitated, fighting back the sobs. "I was too late. Paul had found us. I was devastated when I saw Micky spying on Chandy."

Scott knew the rest of the story. She had told him all about Micky earlier. He just wished he would have caught the creep that day he was peeping in the window. Maybe Chandy would have never been kidnapped if he had. It was all too late now. He just needed to move forward and find a way to rescue Chandy from her horrible Mafia father.

Laura was crying again. "I am so sorry. This is all my fault."

Scott handed her a Kleenex. "No, it's not. Don't think that way, sweetie. You thought you were doing the right thing." He pulled her to her feet and wrapped his arms around her. "I love you." He pulled her away from him and looked deep into her eyes. "I promise we are going to get Chandy back. He can't do this." He picked up the hotel's phone receiver. "I think it is time to let the police know what is going on."

"No!" Laura snatched the receiver. "We can't. Don't you see? I took Chandy away from him and then I faked my own death. Do you know how much trouble I am going to be in?"

Scott knew she was right. He sat on the edge of the bed and thought about what his next move should be. "Okay, I will just go get her myself." He stood to retrieve his clothes out of the closet.

"No, you can't." She glanced outside. "It is already dark out. I think I have a plan that might work."

Scott continued to button up his shirt. "Okay, I'm listening."

"More than likely he has Chandy at his house. It's too late to go there tonight. He has Dobermans and a security system. It would be best if we go in the morning. I know another way to get into the house where the dogs won't even know it. Besides, they wouldn't bother me; I know how to win them over."

Scott interrupted. "Wait a minute. No way. You are not going anywhere! I am not going to lose you again." He kissed her on the forehead. "I will go get our daughter."

"Are you crazy," Laura spat. "He will kill you! You can't go there by yourself. I know—I will go inside and get her while you wait in the car for us. You can park a little way down the street and…."

"No! Absolutely not. I won't let you go, Laura." He threw up his hands. "There is no way you are going there. You give me the address and I will go." He glanced down at his watch. It was after eight. "I will wait and go in the morning when it is light out. He can't hold her against her will. And we both know she don't want to stay there."

Laura shook her head. "You don't have any clue what this man is capable of, do you?"

"Oh, but I do… that is why I'm not letting you go."

"Okay, fine, you go then." She scribbled the address on a napkin. "I'm going to take a shower." Laura picked up her satchel and headed for the bathroom.

She slammed the bathroom door, confirming that she was mad. Scott stared at the closed door. She was just going to have to stay mad because he wasn't going to let her go. He vowed to always protect her, and her daughter and he planned on carrying it through even if it cost him his life.

\*\*\*

Chandy rubbed the sleep out of her eyes and sat up in bed. She didn't know how long she'd been asleep and didn't even remember how she gotten in the room. There was a lamp on a nightstand next to her that had been left on. An unopened bottle of water set next to it. She glanced around the room. It was fashionably decorated in purple and white. The curtains were white with purple stripes. She ran her hand across the fuzzy purple striped bedspread. Over in the corner of the room was a cute white desk with a computer on top. A 26" TV hung on the wall across from the bed. "Wow," she mumbled. More scenic pictures of Italy hung on the walls as well. It was an awesome room. It was almost like he had been expecting her for a while. How could he know her favorite color she wondered?

Paul Gallo's recent words flooded her head. She couldn't believe that he was her father. But she did witness the picture of her mother standing next to him. *What have you done, Mom? Why would you take my away from my biological father?* She instantly remembered being dizzy and unable to stand. He had drugged her. What kind of father would do that? *If he really was her father.*

There was a tap on the door and it cracked open. The woman that had been referred to as Doris peeked in the room. "You're awake." She pushed the door all the way open and entered the room. She stood at the foot of the bed. "Your father would like for you to come back down stairs."

"He's not my father." Chandy couldn't resist the words rushing out. "I already have a father."

Doris looked annoyed. "Mr. Gallo needs to speak to you downstairs now."

She slung her legs over the bed and suddenly realized she was dressed in pajamas. "How did I get these on? I don't remember putting these on."

Doris rolled her eyes and dropped some house slippers on the floor next to her. "Put these on."

Chandy was puzzled but slipped the slippers over her cold bare feet. She wasn't at all impressed with Doris's etiquette. She hadn't been friendly toward her since she'd been there. She acted as thought Chandy was just more work for her to do. All the same, Chandy followed the lady out the door, curious to see what Paul Gallo had to say next. She wondered how long he planned on keeping her here. She was certain her father was worried sick about her. *New York?* She suddenly remembered New York was where her dad had come for his business trip. *Omigod*, she thought, *he could be close by in his hotel.* She wondered if Paul would allow her to call him but instantly thought otherwise. She was certain he wouldn't.

Paul Gallo was in the same chair he was in when Chandy had met him earlier. He stood as she came into the room. "Did you have a nice nap, Chandra?"

"It's Chandy. And you drugged me. Why?"

"You just come right out and speak your mind, don't you, young lady?"

Chandy thought she seen a hint of a grin from the guy for the first time. "I just want answers. Why am I here? And when will you let me go back home."

The grin suddenly disappeared. "First of all, I am your father and you won't carry that tone with me. You are to respect me when you speak to me." His voice was stern, "I will call you Chandra because that is the name I gave you. And I drugged you, so you wouldn't get any wild hair to run off." He walked over to the bar and made a drink. He continued, "You will be staying here from now on. It is time for you to live with me now."

"No!" Chandy snapped. "I don't want to stay with you. I have a father in Missouri that has raised me. He will be worried sick about me."

He glared at her. "Calm down, Chandra, or I will have to give you something else to quiet you down."

Chandy knew he was referring to more drugs. She bit her lip and decided to let him talk. The first chance she got to escape, she would.

"I am gone a lot, so Doris will be looking after you. She will fix your meals and get your clothes ready daily."

*No wonder the woman didn't like me,* Chandy thought. *I am going to be more work for her.*

Paul paused to sip his drink. "Don't think you can run away either." His tone didn't waver, "It's not possible. I am keeping Mick down by the entrance of the gate and I have security cameras all over this place."

Chandy hadn't mentioned her mom since she'd been here but decided to take a risk. "Does my mom know I am here?"

Paul looked shocked at her question. "I imagine she does by now." He sat his glass down and walked toward the window. "Let's just say…if she comes near you, I will kill her!" He spun to stare at Chandy.

The callous look on Paul's face made her cringe. She was convinced that he was serious.

She instantly wished she wouldn't have asked. She decided to change the subject. "What about school? I want to graduate."

"Of course, you do, and you will. There is a private school not far from here that I will get you enrolled in.

Chandy's stomach turned. She felt like she was going to be sick. She didn't want to go to another school. She wanted to be with Kyle and go home to her dad. "But I have a boyfriend back in Missouri. I planned on going to college with him after high school."

"There's no reason for you to go to college. You will never have to work. You will marry Stanton Mozzo after your eightieth birthday. He will take care of you and give you all the money you want. In return, you will do what the rest of the Italian women do and take care of your husband and obey him.

Chandy's mouth dropped. "I'm not marrying him." She couldn't help her outburst, but she wanted to make it clear to him that there was no way in hell she was marrying anyone he instructed her to.

Paul ignored her and yelled for Doris.

Doris entered the room. He instructed her to fix Chandy some dinner and show her around. "I have some errands I need to run."

Paul glared at Chandy, "Don't get cute with Doris either. She can kick your ass if you piss her off. She is currently a black belt and is in better shape than what you think."

Chandy didn't know whether he was telling the truth or if he was bluffing. But she didn't care because she knew the first chance she got, she was escaping. There was no way in hell this vile man was going to keep her here. He would have to kill her first.

## CHAPTER TWENTY

Chandy watched Doris eagerly move around the kitchen, wiping off counters and loading the dishwasher.

She took another bite of the roast beef sandwich that Doris had prepared for her. She didn't realize how hungry she'd been, and frankly, didn't know how long it had been since she'd eaten the sandwich Micky had given her.

Chandy had tried to start a conversation with Doris, but she'd only answer questions with a "yes" or "no" and was very blunt. It was obviously she didn't want to engage in any sort of conversation. So Chandy had given up and ate in silence.

The sound of the back-door slamming made her jump. She glanced over her shoulder at a tall, slender dark-hair guy. He didn't look much older than herself.

He looked startled himself. "Sorry, didn't mean to scare you two. I didn't realize anyone was in here."

Doris glanced toward the front of the house and then back at the boy. Her tone softened, "What are you doing here? You are supposed to be away skiing this weekend."

"It got cancelled," he shrugged. "So here I am." He grinned. "You missed me, didn't you?" He nodded toward Chandy. "So, who's your guest, Doris?"

Chandy instantly noticed how nervous Doris became.

Doris stuttered, "You need to talk to your Dad and he's gone right now. Maybe you should come back later?"

*Dad,* Chandy thought. If she really was Paul Gallo's daughter than this would be a brother of some sort. "I'm Chandy." She didn't wait for Doris to cut her off. She didn't have anything to hide.

"Well nice to meet you, Chandy. My name is Charlie." He held his hand out to shake hers. "Well, that is what they call me anyway. My real name is Paul Charles Gallo." His eyes seemed to question Doris remark. "And I live *here* so why would I leave?"

Doris quickly removed Chandy's plate. "Come on. I need to show you around this place."

"I'm in no hurry," Chandy said. She was really hoping to get to talk to Charlie more. He seemed likeable and maybe he could shed some light on what this was all about.

"Well, I am," Doris snapped. "I have other work to do, so come on."

Chandy didn't think now was the time to disobey Doris, so she stood and followed her toward the kitchen door.

"I'll talk to you later, Chandy." Charlie winked as she walked by.

Doris hadn't seen the wink, but Chandy was certain that Charlie had more to share with her.

\*\*\*

It was after midnight when Chandy heard the tap on her door. She'd almost fallen asleep watching a rerun of *'Friends'*. She jumped up and slipped on the robe Doris had left for her. She was amazed at how the woman had known her size. So far everything she gotten for her had fit perfect.

She cracked the door open to see Charlie grinning at her. She quickly opened the door wider and pulled him into the room. She glanced up and down the hallway and quietly shut the door. "I take it Doris doesn't want you talking to me."

Charlie agreed. "Yeah, that is what I got from the way she was acting. Some strange shit is going on around here." He sat on the edge of the bed. "And I'm dying to know who you are and why you are here." He grinned. "I'm not being rude but I'm nosey as hell." He chuckled. "My first thought was that you were related to Doris but after the way she talked to you...I don't think so any more."

"No, I didn't know her before today."

"Oh," he said with raised eyebrows. "Well, in that case I apologize for her rude behavior. She can be that way sometimes. But sometimes she's not too bad. She's been working for my dad for as long as I can remember."

"So, you live here?" Chandy was eager to confirm what she'd heard earlier in the kitchen.

"I do now. I haven't always though. My grandmother raised me. My mother died giving birth to me. I have only been living with my dad a couple of years now."

"Oh, I'm sorry." Chandy could relate to not having a mom. "Well, I don't know how to tell you this. But your father had me kidnapped!"

"What?" he said a little too loudly. He quickly lowered his voice, "Why would he do that?" He stood and paced in front of the bed. "Don't get me wrong my father isn't any angel." He rolled his eyes. "He's not even close. And he's done a lot of bad things, but I don't understand why he would kidnap you." He faced Chandy. "Usually, he benefits from all his bad doings."

Chandy was having a hard time finding the right words. "Well, he says he is my father?"

"Really?" He looked her up and down as though he hadn't noticed what she looked like before then. "I'm sorry I don't mean to stare, but we are Italian, and you don't look Italian at all."

"I know. I look like my mother. She was fair skin and red hair."

"I'm sorry but I noticed you said *was.* Is she deceased?"

"No, I don't think so. She's been missing for three years. Your father showed me a picture of her; he was standing next to her. And when I asked your father about her now, he talked about her as though she was alive. I think he knows more than he is saying about her whereabouts."

"So, are you saying we could have the same father?" he asked.

"Yes, maybe. But I'm here against my will. And the father that has raised me all these years has to be worried sick."

"I'm sorry my father has brought you here, but I'm sure he has his reasons. He will let you know soon, I'm sure." He shook his head. "I still can't believe I have a sister. I wonder why he never told me." Charlie seemed to be lost in his own thought as he continued, "Maybe because we have never been close. I barely know him...I just know he can be mean." He suddenly glanced up at Chandy. "I'm sorry, I'm just rambling."

"It's okay. I am puzzled too and was hoping you could help me find a way home."

He quickly shook his head. "Oh, I couldn't do that without my father's knowledge. He'd skin me alive. Let's just wait until in the morning and see if we can figure out what is going on."

She was disappointed but could understand his point. "Yes, of course. I'm sorry I asked."

"I'm sure you will be fine. He won't hurt you. He's done a lot of bad things, but I've never known him to hurt a woman." He smiled warmly. "Hey, I'm going to get to my room before Doris makes her rounds. She's known to do that through the night."

"Will I see you in the morning?"

"Sure, you will, sis." He chuckled. "Wow, I love the sound of that. I grew up thinking I was an only child."

"Yeah, me too." She followed him to the door. "Good night." She quietly shut the door. She'd been planning on sneaking out of the house later. She had made friends with Goose and Gator earlier, the Doberman dogs. She'd figured she might be able to sneak by them without them making a fuss, but now she was intrigue with this so-called-brother of hers. She decided she'd have to stick around at least one more day to see what all this fuss was about.

She wished there was a way to contact her dad and Kyle to let them know she was okay. But she didn't have her cell and there didn't seem to be any land lines anywhere in the house. The computer didn't even have the internet; she'd tried that earlier. She wished she'd thought to ask Charlie to use his cell phone. She crawled up in bed and pulled the covers up to her chin. She lied awake for hours thinking about her situation but never could come up with a logical solution for any of this.

***

Laura glanced at the clock on the nightstand—1:15a.m. She silently listened to Scott's heavy breathing. She was certain he was asleep and hopefully he was still a heavy sleeper. There was no way she was going to let him risk his life by going to Paul Gallo's house. Paul would kill him without a second thought and probably right in front of Chandy too. She rolled her eyes as she slipped out of bed. *Hell, he might kill me right in front of my own daughter.* Paul was not a person anyone willingly wanted to confront. If it wasn't for her daughter, she wouldn't dream of going there by herself. But she was certain she was the only one that might even have a chance at rescuing Chandy.

She quickly dressed by the nightlight in the restroom. She scribbled Scott a quick note, explaining why she had to do this alone. She patted her jacket to make sure her pistol was there. She quietly grabbed her helmet and slipped out the door. She was certain that Scott hadn't stirred awake.

\*\*\*

Chandy must have dozed off, but something stirred her awake. She bolted up in bed and listened. All was suddenly quite except for the sound of the TV with another rerun of '*All in the Family*' playing.

There it was again...a creak in the floor like someone walking quietly out in the hallway. She recalled what Charlie had said about Doris making '*her rounds*' through the night. She wondered why she would try to be so sneaky about it though. She probably thought Chandy would try to run off during the night.

There it was again...this time it was a couple of steps and then a couple of more. Chandy was certain someone was out in the hallway now and it seemed as if they were coming closer to her room. She thought about Paul and wondered if he'd come home to check on her. She quickly made her mind up if he knocked on the door she'd pretend to be asleep.

Just then there was a light tap on the door. Chandy froze, uncertain what to do next. She suddenly jumped to her feet. Maybe it was Charlie and he had decided to help her get away after all.

She moved quietly, but swiftly to the door. She pulled the door open a few inches; suddenly, her hand froze on the door knob. She gasped loudly, "Mom?" Even with the chopped off, dark hair Chandy knew it was her.

Laura quickly pushed her way through the slightly opened door and put her finger to her lip, "Shhh." She quietly shut the door behind her.

Chandy was certain she was having one of her nightmares now. No way is her mother that she hadn't seen for three years standing right in front of her, *or is she*?

Laura embraced Chandy tightly and whispered in her ear. "I will explain later. We are in great danger, and I need to get you out of here." She brushed the tears away that were rolling down Chandy's face. "I am so sorry, sweetie. I love you so much and I had to do this for you."

"So, it is true? Paul is my father?" Chandy was in disbelief. "And I have a brother. Why didn't you tell me about Charlie?"

"Charlie?" Laura asked surprised. "I don't know anything about you having a brother. But listen to me now." Her words rushed out, "We need to get out of here, now. You need to do everything I tell you to do and if for any reason we get caught, I will distract attention and you run like hell." She grabbed Chandy's chin and glared into her eyes, "Do you hear me, Chandy?"

The urgency in the way her mother spoke gave her chills. "Mama, I'm scared."

"Just do as I say, baby girl. Now hurry, get dressed."

Chandy quickly slipped into her street clothes. She glanced around the room to see if she had everything, but immediately realized she hadn't anything to leave. She hadn't even asked to come. She followed her mom out in the hallway and briefly thought of Charlie. She thought it was sad how she might not ever see the only brother she had again. "No talking from here on out," her mother whispered, "Just keep right behind me at all times."

Chandy nodded nervously.

She followed her mother down the long hallway and down the stairs, moving as if they were cats on the prowl. She followed her mother into what looked like a den. There was a night light plugged into an outlet that gave up enough light for her to see the books on the shelves, along with a huge desk with a computer on top. Her mom moved toward the already cracked window and opened it more widely. The screen had already been removed. She turned toward Chandy and motioned for her to follow.

Her mother lowered herself through the window and Chandy heard a thump that told her that her mom had hit the ground, so she repeated what she had seen her mother do but falling to her knees instead as she hit the ground. She quickly stood, brushing off the dirt. Gator and Goose had run right up to them, but her mother had already befriended them with comfort words and some treats she had in her pockets.

She whispered to Chandy, "We are going to have to make a run for it down the driveway and up the road around the corner to my bike." She shoved the key in Chandy's hand. "It's red and has a helmet locked in the satchel. "If something should happen, take it, find your dad, and go back to Missouri immediately."

Chandy interrupted. "I know dad is staying at the Holiday Inn on the West side, but I'm not leaving you here, Mom."

She squeezed Chandy's hand. "You have to do what I tell you or he will kill us all. Chandy, I'm not kidding. If you are alive, Paul will more likely keep me alive."

Chandy wasn't sure if she believed all her mom's threatening words but she did believe the seriousness of her voice and knew she should do what her mother told her. "Okay," she promised.

"There are cameras all over this property so when we start running, you need to sprint as fast as you can." She stared at Chandy for a long moment. "I love you, Chandy. Don't ever forget that." She turned back toward Goose and Gator and threw them some more treats. "Let's go."

Chandy's whole body was trembling with fear but she ran as fast as she could right on her mother's heels, down the long-paved driveway.

They had just reached the bottom of the driveway when a long black limousine pulled into the driveway cutting them off.

"Omigod!" Chandy screamed as she came to a sudden halt. They were trapped.

The back-passenger door flew opened and Paul jumped out. A bald, burly man had already jumped out of the driver's side and was running toward Chandy's mother.

Chandy screamed as her mother pulled out a pistol and without delay shot at the driver running toward her. "Run Chandy, run!" her mother shrieked.

Chandy ducked behind the car quickly. She witnessed Paul rushing toward her mother and heard another shot. Chandy glanced long enough to see Paul wresting with her mom, trying to get the gun away.

Chandy took off running before Paul could notice she was gone. She'd never been this scared before in her life—not even when Micky had abducted her. She felt so guilty for not helping her mother, but her mother's instructions kept echoing in her head. She had promised her that she would find her dad. She only prayed that Paul would keep her mom alive while she fetched her father.

She couldn't believe that this was happening. She couldn't believe she actually found her mom and just like that she was gone again. She couldn't stop the tears from falling as the cool wind smacked against her cheeks. *Do the nightmares ever end?* She had no idea how they were going to save her mom from this horrible monster!

CHAPTER TWENTY-ONE

Charlie heard shots and screams nearby. This wasn't unusual for New York, but these sounded closer than usual. He jumped out of bed and ran to the window just in time to witness his dad shoving a dark-head lady into his limousine. His driver, Harry, was clutching his arm. There was blood dripping off his sleeve and Charlie wondered if that was the result of the shots he had heard earlier. He still managed to climb back into the vehicle and drive toward the house.

Charlie slipped on some sweats and hurried down the stairs. Doris was already opening the door. His dad rushed in the house with a firm hold on the lady. He glanced toward Doris, "What the hell happened? I told you to keep an eye on her? And where the hell is Mick?"

"I'm sorry, boss. I must have fallen asleep. I haven't seen Micky tonight."

Charlie stopped at the bottom of the stairs. He was almost scared to speak; his dad looked so angry. "Everything okay?" he finally asked. He followed him into the front room.

Paul jerked his head toward Charlie as if he hadn't noticed him before. "What the hell are you doing here? I thought you were gone for the weekend."

"My trip got cancelled."

Paul turned his attention back to Doris. "Quick, Harry needs help. He's been shot."

"Yes, boss." She pushed Harry toward the back of the house.

The lady continued to plea with his father, "Please just let me go. I won't say anything to anyone. I promise. I just want you to leave me and my daughter alone."

Charlie winced as his dad smacked the lady across the face. "Shut up," he screamed.

Charlie had heard horrid stories about his dad's violent nature, but he had never witnessed his dad in any such manner until now.

He'd never feared his dad before but suddenly he did. The way in which he was treating the lady made him think that maybe Chandy had been telling the truth about his father. And maybe something more was going on here that he wasn't aware of.

His father grabbed the lady's shoulder and shoved her forcefully down on the couch. "Charlie, stay with her. I'm locking you in here with her until I get back."

"What is going on, Dad?"

His dad's eyes narrowed. "Just do as I say. You hear? I'll explain later." He tucked the gun he was holding into his pants. "I will leave Jimmy outside to watch the door in case the bitch tries to get cute."

He rushed toward the door but turned and glared at the lady with one of the coldest looks Charlie had ever seen his father give anyone. He snapped, "I will give Jimmy permission to kill you if you try to escape." With that said he exited out of the room, slamming the door behind him.

Charlie was stunned at his father's harsh words and he instantly felt sorry for this strange lady. She was shaking her head and bawling uncontrollably.

Charlie's inner compassion kicked in. He didn't care who she was; he wasn't going to continue to treat her badly like he had just witnessed his father doing. He reached for some tissues on the end of the table and rushed over to her side. "Here is some Kleenex. I am so sorry for the way my father just treated you."

The lady looked up at him and took the tissue. "Your father?"

He nodded.

"You can call me Laura." She hesitated, as if searching for the right words to speak, "You need to help me, please. My daughter, Chandy is in danger."

"Chandy?" *This was Chandy's long lost missing mother?* He knew it; his sister *was* involved in this mess somehow. Now the lady had his full attention. As scared as he was of his father, meeting Chandy and knowing he had a real sister had made him feel more alive than he ever had before. Those few moments he had spent with Chandy had been so genuine and the bond he had instantly felt with her was real. He knew she was truly his sister. What he didn't understand is why they had been kept apart all these years. He wasn't going to turn his back on his sister...not now.

He turned his attention back to Laura. He knew he was taking a big risk going against his father's demands, but he was willing to help her if it meant helping his sister. He may find out sooner than he wanted how vile a man his father can be.

*\*\**

Chandy had never ran so fast and hard in her life. Every few seconds she would glance over her shoulder to make sure her 'so call' father hadn't caught up with her. Luckily, the sun hadn't come up yet, so she could still hide between the towering buildings as cars passed by. She had first run toward the motorcycle like her mother had told her but there was just one problem, Chandy had no idea had to ride the bike and quickly realized now wasn't the time to learn. She didn't ponder with her decision; she ran on by and kept running. All she needed to do was find her dad's hotel or even a phone to call him. She didn't have any money for a taxi. She knew the city was huge and she could be miles from the hotel. Her best bet would be to keep on the run until a local store opened and then use someone's cell phone to call her dad.

After several blocks, her panting increased to a point where she thought she might throw up, so she slowed her pace down. She had no clue what time of the morning it was, but she did notice it was starting to get slightly lighter out. Sirens could be heard in the distant. She only wished she would run into a policeman. She glanced around at her surroundings. There was a cluster of tall apartment buildings all around. She seemed to be a good area which made her feel a little safer. She noticed a couple of lights on in some of the apartments, but most of them remained dark. She was too terrified to try knocking on any of the doors. Besides, most of them had lobbies entrances, and she was certain they would probably all be locked up. She would have to be very careful who she asked for help from.  After all, this was still New York City and known for their high crime rate. She didn't want to be just another statistic. She brushed away a tear. She didn't have time to be emotional. She had to stay strong; she had a mother to save.

***

Scott glanced at the clock on the night stand. It was 5:40am. He had slept soundly through the night. He usually woke up three or four times during the night, but his lack of sleep must have caught up with him. He flipped over to cuddle with Laura before taking his shower, but the bed was empty. His first thought was she was already in the shower. So, he laid there for a few minutes waiting for her to come out of the bathroom. All of a sudden, he realized it was just too quiet, and he recalled her taking a shower before she'd gone to bed. He jumped out of bed and ran to the bathroom. But he knew before he even opened the door that she wasn't going to be in there. He scanned the room for her helmet. It was also gone.

He slammed his fist on the dresser. "Damn it, Laura!" He knew exactly where she went before he even saw the note on the table. He was certain she'd had her mind made up when she'd went to bed last night that she was going to Paul's house to get Chandy. He couldn't stop the tears. "Omigod, I can't lose you again!" Now, not only was his daughter in danger, but his wife was gone *again.* He quickly dressed and paced back and forth in front of the window debating what to do. Although Laura had warned him about getting the police involved, he just didn't think he had much of an option. If this man was as dangerous as Laura says, maybe it was time to get the police involved.

Suddenly, he thought of Sam Rivers, a longtime friend of his from high school, who had gone to work for the FBI a few years ago. Although Scott hadn't talked to him for a while, he had heard that he was working somewhere in New York. "I can't believe I didn't think of this sooner," he said out loud. Scott was trying not to get his hopes up but was really hoping Sam was working in New York City. He searched the Internet until he located a phone number for him and quickly dialed it. He prayed silently as the phone rang. This was his last hope for saving his wife and daughter.

***

Chandy knelt behind a car until the approaching black car had gone by. Now it was light out and traffic was picking up fast. She was having a hard time finding places to hide and there were just too many cars to hide from every one of them. She was glad she was in a good area and some of the shops were starting to open. People were starting to flood the sidewalks. She was glad she could blend in with the crowd. She knew it would be super hard for Paul to find her now.

She saw a lady flip the sign over from *'Closed'* to *'Open'* in a nearby salon. She quickly rushed in the place not sure what she was going to say. She decided not to say too much.

"Hi, Ma'am. I'm sorry to bother you so early, but I'm kind of lost. I lost my cell phone and was wondering if I could use a phone to call my father," she was so anxious that she didn't even breath in between sentences.

The lady looked hesitant but finally nodded to a phone on the counter. "You can use that one there. But make it quick. It is our business phone." The lady grabbed a broom out of the corner and continued to sweep around the salon.

The phone had only rung once and Chandy heard her father on the other end.

"Hello."

Her heart melted at the sound of his voice. Emotion overwhelmed her. "Dad," she cried. "Omigod, Dad. I've been so scared. I escaped, but now he has mom."

"Oh Chan, thank God. Are you okay?"

"I'm fine but mom's alive and he has her."

The lady sweeping the floor cleared her throat to get Chandy's attention. "I'm sorry, Ma'am. Just a second and I will be done."

She turned her attention back to her dad. "I got to get off here. Can you come and get me?"

"Where you at baby girl?"

Chandy glanced back toward the woman and covered the mouthpiece. "What is the name of this place?"

The lady looked hesitant once again but answered, "Sherie and PJ's Salon."

Chandy repeated back into the phone, "Sherie and PJ's Salon." The lady gave her the address and Chandy repeated it back to her dad.

"Stay there. I'm on my way," her dad said.

"What about Mom?" she asked eagerly.

"We are going to get her. No one is going to keep us from being a family. Hang tight, baby girl. I'm on my way." With those words, her dad hung up.

## CHAPTER TWENTY-TWO

Micky swore under his breath as he pulled into the driveway. "Sonofabitch!" All the lights were on in the courtyard and the dogs were pacing back and forth, barking. Something was going on and he'd only left his post for ten minutes to go get a sandwich. "Damn!" He knew he was in trouble if something bad had happened. He feared that the girl had tried to escape. Paul would kill him if she did get away!

His cell phone rang, and he knew it was him before he even looked at it. "Boss? What's going on? I just ran down to get a sandwich…"

"Would you shut the fuck up and listen to me before I fucking blow your stupid head off, you idiot!"

"Sorry, boss."

"She's gone and it's all your fucking fault. I have her crazy-ass mom at the house. But I don't want her; I want my daughter! If you want to save your ass you better find her," he screamed. "I'm covering the west side, you take the east side. She can't be far because she's on foot. And I want her alive so don't get cute!"

"I'm on it now." Micky hung up and hurriedly circled around the driveway and back out onto the street.

"Stupid bitch is going to get my head blown off," he mumbled. He'd witness his boss kill his workers before for not following orders—he knew he was no exception. *He will probably kill me even if I bring the bitch back,* he thought. He hit the steering wheel with his fist. "Sonofabitch," he said again. "I can't go back there."

"I'm a dead man if I do," he said aloud. Micky continued to drive up and down the streets, looking for the girl as his mind raced what he should do. He had never really thought to cross Paul Gallo because of his status with the Mafia. No one messes with Paul Gallo and lives to tell about it. But what if he did and could pull it off? He knew his boss had more money than he could ever spend in a lifetime. "But does he give me a raise? Hell no," he sputtered loudly.

And Micky knew a couple of guys that would give anything to get even with Paul Gallo. *Omigod,* he thought. *Do I dare?* He knew if he didn't try...he would be dead by this time tomorrow morning. His mind was made up. He knew he didn't have anything to lose. But first he had to find the girl before his boss did!

\*\*\*

Chandy crossed her arms and stood under the awning of the salon. She had waited inside for a while, but the lady kept making snide remarks as if she didn't want her in there. Chandy decided to wait in front of the shop and hoped she didn't have to wait long for her father.

The salon was in the center of a side street. There were clothes shops on each side of the salon and a book store further down on the corner. Although it was busy avenue, it wasn't as bad as a lot of the New York streets. It was still early, slightly after seven, so a lot of the shops still weren't open yet.

Chandy was expecting her father to pull up in a taxi since he didn't have any other transportation that she knew of. Every time a taxi pulled up near the shop, she would get excited only to be let down. Apparently, a lot of people took taxies to work. Although it had only been ten or so minutes since she talked to her father, she was anxious to see him. She was so worried about her mother and what was happening to her.

She waited another ten minutes impatiently pacing in front of the shop. Finally, a taxi pulled up across the street, and she saw him get out. He waved anxiously and leaned back into to talk to the taxi driver.

A sudden jab in her back startled her.

"Don't say a word," he hissed.

She shuddered in fear. She instantly recognized the voice and knew the point in her back was from the gun of the man that had kidnapped her.

It all happened so fast. The guy shoved her into the car that was pulled up near the curb. She saw her father trying to get through the traffic to reach her. "You make the wrong move and I will shoot your dad right here!" He slammed her door shut and ran around to jump into the driver's side.

She could hear her dad yelling at the top of his lungs, "Stop that man! He has my daughter! Someone call the police. Chandy...Chandy.... let her go!"

She choked back tears as her father screams grew fainter as the man sped down the street. She couldn't resist glancing over her shoulder toward her dad. He was still chasing the vehicle, although, he was getting further and further away.

"Please, let me go with my dad. Please, don't take me back there," she pleaded. She knew what the answer would be, but she had to try.

"Shut up."

The guy had sweat dripping off his forehead although it wasn't even warm out. He looked even rougher than he had the last time she had seen him. His eyes were bloodshot as though he either hadn't had any sleep or was on drugs. The thought frightened her even more. She heard horrid stories of people on drugs. She glanced toward the door handle—she debated rather to try jumping out.

It was as though the thug read her mind. "Don't even think about it, Missy." He pointed the gun toward her head. "I'll blow your head off right here. And nobody would think anything of it because gun shots go off all the time in this city."

She glanced toward all the people rushing up and down the sidewalks and quickly decided that he was probably right. They all seemed to be in their own little world with their own little problems. *But none as big as mine right now,* she thought. Even if she screamed they probably wouldn't even acknowledge her. She had never felt so helpless in her life. She couldn't stop the sobs and she didn't care. If the loathsome man didn't like it, he could just shoot her; she'd probably be better off dead anyway than living with her real father!

***

Laura's head was spinning. She couldn't believe she'd been

caught. *How could I have been so careless? And I shot a yard*

*ornament, for crying out loud. I was aiming at the idiot's head,* she thought silently. She couldn't believe it! How could she have messed up something so important?

Her life didn't matter to her at this point. But Chandy's did. Everything she had done thus far, she had done to save Chandy from this evil man. She gave up three years of her life—three years that she could have been enjoying her husband and her daughter. She missed out on all the dances, the boyfriends, the track meets. She broke her daughter and her husband's hearts. And now none of it matter. She bowed her head and sobbed louder. "It's useless."

The boy returns from the bar and hands Laura a bottle of water. "Here, try to drink this."

"Thank you." She lifted her head and took the bottle of water. She blew her nose and cleared her throat. "I'm sorry, but what was your name?"

"Charlie Gallo. Paul is my father. And Chandy says it is her father also—which if that is true that would make her my sister."

188

"Unfortunately, it is true. Paul Gallo is Chandy's biological father. I was once married to your father, but I left when Chandy was just an infant. She was raised by another man that loves her as his own, and she grew up thinking Scott Hayes was her father." Her voice cracked, "Omigod what have I done. I have made a mess of things."

"I'm kind of confused with the story," Charlie admitted. "But I want to help you if I can."

*Charlie,* Laura thought silently. She recalled Chandy saying she had a brother named Charlie, but she had her mind on escaping at the time and didn't think too much about it. "How old are you Charlie?"

"I'm seventeen."

"Really? So is Chandy." This really didn't surprise Laura. She knew that Paul had many women while they were married. She could have cared less. The more he was with other women, the less he wanted her and that was what she had wanted!

"When is your birthday," she asked.

"I was born here in New York on October 9, 1995."

"Omigod. How bizarre. Chandy's birthday is October 8th. You two were born a day apart.

Charlie looked baffled. "But how can that be if you were married to my dad at the time?"

Laura grinned. "Ummm, what do you think?"

He looked confused. "But my father said he was married to my mother and she died at child birth."

"Forgive my bluntness but your father is nothing more than an evil, lying bastard!" She shook her head. "Your father had many women while we were married."

189

"I'm sorry you had to go through that." Charlie added, "I've only been living with my father the last couple of years. My grandma raised me because my father *was and still is* so busy with his work. But now that I'm older and can take care of myself, he thought it was time for me to come to live with him."

"And how has that been for you?"

"Well, with me in school and him working, I can honestly say I don't know him any better than I did when I lived with my grandma."

Laura felt sorry for the kid. And although she thought it was odd for him to confess his true feelings to a strange woman, she didn't blame him. She could remember how lonely she felt as Paul's wife.

Laura stood and glanced around at the room, trying to find a way to get out. She suddenly felt that she really could trust the kid. He didn't seem like he was Mafia, although she knew he was by blood. She didn't think he had it in him to carry out some of the malice acts his father would expect from him.

"I need to find Chandy before your father does. Will you help me, Charlie?"

"If I can, I most certainly will. I will pay the consequences later."

"Your father used to have a key rack with keys to every door and window in this house. Does he still have it?"

"Wow, I'm not aware of any key rack."

She ran over to the window behind the bar. It was high up, so she climbed on one of the bar stools. She unlocked and tried to lift it up, but it wouldn't budge.

"Omigod! What did your father do glue the windows down?"

"Here let me try." Charlie climbed up on another bar stool and tried to lift the window up. With no luck, he jumped back off the barstool and tried a different window across the room, but the same thing. "I guess he really didn't trust me to keep watch on you." He shook his head. "I don't know what else to do."

"The window in the den came right up. I didn't have any trouble breaking into the house to get me daughter." Then it hit her. He had known she would come. He purposely left the window unlocked in hopes of catching her. "Damn it," she said under her breath.

"Let's just wait for my father and I will try talking to him."

Laura knew she didn't have any other options, but was sure that there wasn't anything that Charlie could say that would change his father's mind on Laura's future fate.

*** 

Scott was furious. He yelled, not to anyone in particular, but at the crowd that had started to gather around him, "Why didn't anyone stop him? He took my daughter." He shook his head in disbelief. "And not one of you tried to help. Could you not hear me screaming?" He nodded toward the guy who had paused from washing windows. "You were five feet from her and you didn't even try to stop the guy! Why?" The guy turned back around toward the windows and continued washing as if he didn't hear a word. Scott threw his hands up, "Omigod, I don't get it!"

Only one gray-headed elderly lady in a fancy suit acknowledged him. She handed him a business card. "You can try calling the police. They might help you if they have time. But if not, here's a private investigator that I personally know. He will help you." She spun on her high-heels and hurried on across the street.

Scott sighed in frustration and made his way back to the taxi that he had waiting. He knew there was no way they would be able to catch up with the hoodlum.

He was thankful that he had gotten a hold of Sam Rivers earlier and was thrilled to find out that his friend had an office a few miles away from his hotel. The only thing was he currently had other obligations and couldn't meet with him until after lunch.

Scott couldn't wait any longer. He decided he would have to go to Paul Gallo's house by himself. He dialed Sam River's number as his taxi pulled into the jammed-packed traffic.

At first, his friend begged him not to do anything yet. But when Scott explained to him exactly what just happened to his daughter, right in front of his eyes, Sam agreed to meet with him immediately if he would hold off on going to the Gallo's house by himself. He informed Scott if he made the wrong move it could cost some lives. Scott reluctantly agreed; he knew Sam was right. They decided to meet at a little coffee shop a few blocks away from the Gallo house. He rattled off the address to the taxi as he fought back the tears. He was so close to having a breakdown. He didn't know how much longer he could hold it together. But he took a deep breath. He knew he had to keep it together for *his* wife and daughter!

CHAPTER TWENTY-THREE

It was different than the time before; Chandy was more scared than ever now. Micky had punched her and smacked her around. He had also suggested he was going to do sexual acts with her later. She shuddered with the horrible thought. For whatever reason, Micky didn't seem as patient and seemed so much crueler than the first time he kidnapped her. Although at the time, she didn't believe he could be any more despicable. His demeanor had definitely changed for the worse. She had assumed he would take her right back to Paul Gallo's house, but he hadn't. He had taken her to a shabby hotel room and had tied her up. He threatened to kill her right there if she screamed. She was certain that Paul Gallo wouldn't have told him to do that.

He paced nervously back and forth in front of the window. He suddenly snatched his cell phone off the TV and made a call. Chandy listened fearfully to the one-sided conversation.

"Hey Lester, it's Mick. Well, it's done. I have her." He snickered. "What do you mean you didn't think I had it in me? I'm tired of being dicked around by that jerk.

I tend to make him pay for all the fucked-up jobs he made me do for him." He rubbed his hands anxiously through his hair. "So, you want a piece of the pie?" He glanced down at his watch. "Okay, thirty minutes. See you then."

Chandy trembled as he circled around her. She didn't like the sound of the conversation.

Micky tugged on her ropes and then tied the chair to the desk. He stuffed some cloth into her mouth. She knew better than to resist because the last time she tried to break away from him he had hit her hard. He hadn't offered her food or water like the time before either. He was definitely up to something that terrified her.

"I expect you to be in the same position when I get back. If the chair has moved an inch, I will know and there will be hell to pay for it. Do you understand, little rich girl?"

She wanted to shout, *I'm not rich and Paul Gallo is not my father. And I don't want to be here. I want to go home to my country home in Missouri with my mom and dad.* But being gagged, she could only nod.

He tucked the pistol into his jeans, grabbed his cell phone, and shoved it into his jean's pocket. He pulled back the drapes and glanced up and down the street before silently slipping out the door, leaving Chandy tied up in the dreadful room. She heard him lock the door from the outside and pull on the knob to make sure it locked.

The tears were burning behind her eyelids, but she knew now wasn't the time to cry. This was a matter of life and death and her only chance to escape. Her eyes darted uneasily around the room, searching for an answer to this horrible situation.

*** 

Laura jumped up from the couch as Paul entered the room. Her whole body was trembling—she folded her arms across her chest, hoping to disguise her fear. She glanced toward Charlie, hoping he'd be some kind of moral support if needed. His dark piercing eyes were focused on his father. She knew at that moment he could never go against his father's wishes. As much as she would like to think he would help her if needed, she knew he didn't have it in him. He wasn't at all like these other vicious men; she couldn't believe that he could be Paul's son. He was nothing like him at all.

Following close behind Paul were three brawny Italian men. Two of them looked younger than her, but the third one she recognized from all those years ago. They called him Ratty. Of course, he was much younger then. She recalled the scar across his nose and the tattoo of a black rat slivering up his arm. She was certain that is where his nickname came from. She had never personally talked to him, but he'd hung around a lot. She always thought of him as one's of Paul's bodyguards. She was always scared of him. *Hell, she feared all Paul's men.* And she had every right to be. She knew how violent the Mafia was. She had blocked out many of the horrible memories that she'd witness. These vile men didn't have a problem expressing their hatred anywhere and anytime. And if you tried to double cross them they would torture you even worse. That thought terrified her. She knew Paul would kill her for what she had done to him. It was just a matter of *when* he would do it.

It was her daughter she feared for and the life she would have if she had to spend it with her biological father. The thought of Chandy having to marry one of those horrible Mafia guys sent chills up and down her spine.

Paul crossed the room to the bar and made a drink. He sipped his drink and slowly made his way back across the room. He spoke to Charlie first. "Did she give you any trouble or try to escape?"

"No, Sir."

Laura was thankful for Charlie's lie.

Paul's eyes narrowed as they met Laura's. "So where did you send Chandy to?"

"I don't know what you're talking about," she responded. *Thank you, God,* she thought silently. She was thrilled he hadn't found her. No way in hell was she going to tell him anything.

He grabbed a handful of hair and jerked her head back. "Anyone tell you that you look hideous as a brunette? Now, where is she?"

She grinded her teeth together trying to hide the pain. "I don't know where she went. I told her to run."

His grip tightened, and she winced.

"Dad, maybe she will come back soon." Charlie quickly added, "She doesn't know anyone in this city."

Laura knew Charlie's words were for her own sake. But that didn't lessen the grip Paul had on her hair. "Where's Scott staying?" He suddenly let loose of her hair and shoved her down to the couch.

"You leave him out of this. He has nothing to do with any of this. He doesn't even know Chandy's here. And he thinks I'm dead."

"You know, Shannon, I don't believe anything you say! Or is it Laura now?"

She didn't respond.

"Charlie, come over here." Paul motioned for him to stand next to him. "I think it is time you man up and become one of us."

Laura felt bad for the kid. He looked like he had just seen a ghost. But he did as his father told him.

"Torch, come here!"

The hefty bald guy looked surprised, "Me, boss?"

"Yes, you!" Paul rolled his eyes.

Torch hesitated and then slowly walked toward his boss. "Yes boss?"

Paul casually sipped his drink. "I left something in the pool house at back. It was in a drawer in the desk where my computer sets." Paul shrugged his shoulders. "It's gone now!"

Torch's face turned white.

Paul continued, "Doris said you were out there yesterday. Did you take something out of my desk, Torch?"

Torch stuttered, "I was going to put it back. I was going to tell you that I took it, but you were gone." He popped his knuckles nervously. "Really, boss, I was going to put it back."

"When?"

"As soon as I could get some money to repay you. I will, boss, I promise. I would never steal from you, boss."

Laura actually felt sorry for the guy. He was shaking worse than she was.

Suddenly, Paul jerked his gun from his pants and poked the barrel in Torch's chest. "No one fucking steals from Paul Gallo!" Without any hesitation, he pulled the trigger.

Laura screamed as Torch clutched his chest. Another shot rang out and Torch hit the floor.

Paul turned toward Charlie, "And that my son is what happens when someone tries to screw over a Gallo!"

"Omigod, Dad!" Charlie's mouth hung open.

"Ratty, Wes, get rid of him and get this mess cleaned up"

The other two rushed over and quickly picked up the body. Ratty looped his arms under Torche's armpits, while Wes snatched his legs. They carried him out of the room.

"Tell Doris I will need her assistance here shortly." Paul glanced back toward the men. "So, you both do know to never take anything that doesn't belong to you, right?"

Simultaneously the guys quickly replied, "Yes, boss."

"Shut the door when you leave and wait outside when you're done."

The guys eagerly nodded and continued carrying the dead guy out.

For some reason his recent actions terrified Laura. She didn't know what his next plans were, but she was certain that he was trying to make a point to Charlie about people taking anything from a Gallo. She was sure he was referring to her, taking Chandy away from him.

"See this lady here." Paul told Charlie. "I was married to her at one time."

Charlie pretended to be surprised.

"Yes, and when a woman marries into the Mafia family she becomes property of the husband." He patted Charlie on the back. "I know that you haven't been around much because of school and living with grandma. I've missed out on teaching you a lot of the Mafia's ways, and I hope I'm not too late—because one day you will have to take over for me. And I know you will make me proud." He grinned. "Because after all, you are a Gallo and you represent, right?" He held his hand up for Charlie to smack.

Charlie hesitated briefly before following suit and smacking his father's hand. "I will try to represent the best I can."

"Well then your first task is about to happen."

*Omigod,* Laura thought, *what is he going to make him do? Poor kid.*

"Well, this woman here stole my only daughter from me and kept her away from me for seventeen years."

Charlie spoke nervously, "Yeah, but Chandy is back now." He hesitated. "And she can live with us for now on, right?" He took a deep breath, "So you did win after all."

"But your first lesson—no one takes anything from a Gallo without being punished."

"What do you mean?" He nervously looked toward the lady. "I don't think you should kill her." He quickly shook his head. "No Dad, that would upset Chandy really bad."

Laura stiffened; she wasn't surprised. He wasn't even going to wait until he got Chandy back. He was going to kill her now.

"Oh, you are so right, my son, it would definitely upset Chandy if I killed her mom; she would never forgive me. And I don't want any blood on my hands for killing her mother. *This* will be your first assignment." He pushed the gun toward Charlie to take. "You kill her!"

Laura was speechless. *Omigod! How could he ask his own son to do such a thing? What a scumbag!*

"No, Dad, I won't do it," Charlie stuttered.

Paul's eyes narrowed. "What do you mean you won't do it? I'm not asking you, son—I'm telling you!"

"I'm not killing her!" He folded his arms across his chest and his eyes met his father's. "I'm not killing her or anyone else for that matter! Ever! If I must kill someone to be a Gallo, then I don't want to be a part of this family."

"You don't have a choice. You either learn to kill or there will be consequences that I personally don't want to deal with."

"No, Dad. I like this lady, and I don't have anything against her. She hasn't done anything wrong. And I like my sister that I never knew I had. Chandy hasn't seen her mother for three years. If you kill her," he cleared his throat and spoke in a harsh voice. "I will go to the police."

"What the hell! Are you threatening me, Charlie?"

Paul's face was beet red, and Laura knew he was mad as hell and she was horrified! "Stop, Paul. Leave the kid alone and kill me yourself! You are a coward if you have to have the boy do it for you!"

Paul backhanded her across the face.

Laura winced and grabbed her cheek.

He bent forward until his eyes were a couple inches away from hers. "You know what.... I have a better plan. I am going to make you pay in the worse way, bitch! You are going to kill Charlie, so I don't have to."

"What? You are fucking insane!" Laura added, "I won't do any such thing."

Charlie shook his head in disbelief. "You would kill your own son?"

"Of course not! I just said I wouldn't do that! I'm going to have your own *mother* do it!" He glared at Laura.

It took Laura a few seconds to realize what he was saying. "What the hell are you talking about?" she asked puzzled.

Charlie chimed in, "You said my mom died at childbirth." He stared at Laura as if he was trying to figure out if his dad was telling the truth.

"You had twins." A devious grin spread across Paul's face.

"That's impossible." Laura didn't believe him. "The doctor told me there was only one."

Paul laughed callously. "He was *my* doctor, you idiot. Yes, my doctor, my hospital, my money!" He laughed out loud and lit a cigarette. He took a few puffs off the cigarette, all the while the smirk never left his face. He seemed to be enjoying torturing Laura.

Laura couldn't believe her ears. This surely couldn't be true. She would have known if she was carrying twins at some time.

"Did you really think you needed a C-Section?" Paul laughed again. "It was all part of the plan. I knew there was a boy and a girl. I had Charlie stay at my mother's place, so you would never know." He shook his finger at her. "See, I knew you would try to run off. I just didn't think you would succeed at it."

"You bastard!" Laura screamed.

Charlie fell to his knees. Tears were streaming down his cheeks. He stared at Laura. "All these years I thought my mom died having me?" His eyes darted back to his dad. "How could you? You took my sister and *my mom*!" He glared up at his dad. "You are the worst father a son could have!"

"I know." He grinned and pushed the gun toward Laura. "Now kill your son!"

"Fuck you! I won't do no such thing!"

He laughed heartlessly.

Laura knew he was enjoying the torment. "You are sick!"

Paul started to respond but his cell phone rung and he pulled it out and glanced at the caller ID. His face suddenly turned serious and he quickly answered, "Mick, about damn time. Did you find her?"

He paused. "What? What the hell are you talking about, you damn fool," he shouted. "I will find you and personally cut your fucking balls off!" He shoved his phone in his pocket. "Doris!" he yelled out the door. "Get Wes and Ratty! Tell them to hurry." He glanced back towards Laura and Charlie. "We will finish this when I get back."

"Doris, make sure this door is locked and neither one of them leave!" He stopped in front of her. "Can you do that right this time?"

"Yes, boss!"

He hurriedly tucked his gun in his pants and flew out the door.

## CHAPTER TWENTY-FOUR

Chandy had tried to loosen the ropes but was unsuccessful. She grunted angrily; she was getting discouraged. However, she did manage to get the rope a little looser around her ankles. She thought if she had more time she would be able to get at least one foot out, but by then Micky would be back. She had heard him tell the guy on the phone thirty minutes which she assumed was the time they were meeting. She was sure ten minutes had already passed. She glanced toward the phone on the nightstand, but even if she got the chair loose and managed to jump somehow over there, it would still be useless. She could turn the chair around and dial, but she wouldn't be able to talk with the damn gag in her mouth. She quickly tossed that idea out of her head.

Suddenly, she heard footsteps approaching. It sounded like someone was right outside the door. She remained silent. She prayed it wasn't Micky back so soon.

There was tap on the door. Then a lady in a small voice said, "Housekeeping. I have more clean towels for you."

*Omigod, please, please, please come in,* Chandy silently prayed.

Chandy heard the key in the door and watched as the doorknob turned. She held her breath and prayed it wasn't some kind of sick joke.

A petite Asian lady entered carrying a handful of towels. She screamed when she saw Chandy tied up in the chair.

Chandy watched helplessly as the lady threw the towels on the bed. She started to turn and leave but immediately turned back toward Chandy. "Are you okay?" She glanced nervously around the room.

Chandy shook her head vigorously!

The lady pulled the gag out of her mouth. "Should I call the police."

"Yes, but untie me first please."

The lady fussed with the knots and eventually got them all untied. She looked nervously over her shoulder. "I better go. I will call the police for you." She rushed out of the room.

"Thank you, thank you so much," Chandy called after her. She quickly followed the woman out the door. She scanned the parking lot, looking for Micky's car. She sighed in relief. It was nowhere around. She wasn't sticking around for the police. She'd heard horror stories on New York police and how long it takes to get help. Hopefully, they would show up about the time that Micky got back and then they could arrest him, although the victim would be long gone.

She glanced around at her surroundings. She needed to call her dad, but now wasn't the time. The motel was called "The Forest Inn." *Funny name for a motel that doesn't have any trees around it,* she thought briefly. She glanced at other landmarks as she ran across the parking lot. She quickly ducked behind a car as a car approached the entrance of the motel. She glanced around at the area. It looked to be on the outskirts of New York City, she thought—maybe a suburb. There wasn't as much traffic or as many businesses. There was a Longhorn Steak house on one side of the motel and a gas station on the other. There were fast food joints all along the highway. She thought she could make it to the gas station and call her dad but quickly dismissed the idea—it was still too close. She needed to run as far as she could before calling him.

She hurriedly sprinted down the driveway. A dark blue BMW turned into the driveway. Luckily, she didn't recognize the vehicle which she was thankful for because there was nowhere to hide at this point.

The driver rolled down the window. "Are you okay, Miss?"

The windows were tinted so she wasn't sure who else was in the car with the guy. She knew it was dangerous to take rides from stranger, but she also knew Micky should be coming back at any time. She didn't have time to think about it. "I'm in a lot of trouble. I've been kidnapped." The words rushed out as the tears flowed freely down her cheeks. "The man is coming back for me because he thinks I'm still tied up in the motel room. Could you please take me to the police station?"

"Why of course, I will—jump in the back seat."

The man seemed sincere, and Chandy was relieved to find someone to help her. She opened the door and quickly crawled in. She gasped when her eyes met the man next to her. It was her biological father, Paul Gallo. "Let me out." She screamed and reached for the door handle. But it was too late. The door was locked.

She was trapped. *How the hell could this be happening again? Omigod I can't take it!* She bowed her head and cried.

Paul ordered the driver to pull down to the motel. He asked Chandy, "Which room did Mick have you in."

She refused to answer him. She would ignore him and act like he didn't exist. Unless…. "Where's my mom?"

"Your mom is fine." He grinned. "For now, that is." He ordered the driver, "Drive down into the parking lot and look for his car."

"Please don't hurt my mom. I will tell you which room if you promise not to hurt her."

"Child, I don't need your help. We easily traced him here by his cell phone. I'm sure we can at least figure out what room he was in."

Chandy could care less what happened to Micky. She was almost certain by the conversation she heard that he wasn't working with Paul but maybe plotting against him. As much as she didn't want to be with Paul she felt somewhat safer with him than with

Micky. She was certain Micky would had eventually raped her and probably killed her too. "That's the room." She pointed to the room that she had just escaped from. She heard sirens in the distance and suddenly perked up. Maybe, the lady had called the police and that was them coming. But the sirens faded away along with her hope. She knew it was time for Micky to come back and it was possible he would bring the guy that he was talking to on the phone. She didn't want to be anywhere around if these thugs had a shootout. She decided to volunteer Micky's intentions. "Micky went to meet a guy named Lester. He had me tied to a chair, and I heard him say he would be back in thirty minutes."

Paul seemed to be impressed. "You escaped? Good girl." He patted her leg.

"No. A lady in housekeeping came by with some clean towels and she untied me." She left out the part about the lady supposing to call the police.

The guy in the front passenger side chuckled. "Micky's such a loser!"

Paul quickly called someone on his cell phone. "Darrel, he's in number 18. I want you and Chuck to go inside and be waiting for him when he gets back there." He continued, emphasizing his words, "And I don't want him left alive. Is that understood?"

There was a short pause. "Make sure of it then. Okay, I will see you back at the house."

Paul yelled at the driver. "Turn this sucker around." He smiled at Chandy. "I need to take my daughter home."

Chandy cringed at the thought. She wanted to scream *I'm not your daughter* but decided against it. She had a sinking feeling her life would never be the same again!

***

Scott told Sam the whole story even about his wife's fake disappearance. He knew he was taking a big risk because Laura could be jailed for what she did. But Sam had actually been more understanding than he thought. Sam's main concerned was capturing Paul Gallo.

Sam wiped his brow with his handkerchief. "Do you know how long I've been trying to nail that scumbag?" The guy shook his head. "He's one of the biggest Mafia leaders in New York City."

"What about the guy that has Chandy? You think he is taking her back to the Gallo's house."

"I imagine it is one of Paul's men. Hopefully, Chandy is with your wife now. But we can't act until I have all my backup in place. My boys are getting a search warrant now. We want to do everything legal, so it all don't get tossed out." He glanced at his watch. "It shouldn't be much longer now."

Scott held his hand out to shake Sam's. "Thanks so much, Sam. I didn't know who to go to."

"You did the right thing. You couldn't handle Paul Gallo by yourself. No one can, believe me. He has way too many men working for him. He probably owns half the city." He sighed. "Well, maybe not that much but he does own a lot of businesses.

"I know your right," Scott admitted. "I was thinking about trying to rescue my family myself, but I would have probably been killed."

"More than likely." He grinned. "Come' on, let's go over and stake out the house until our back up gets there."

"I'm so nervous!" Scott wiped his palms on his jeans.

"I promise, I will do everything in my power to get your wife and daughter back to you."

"I know," Scott said. But all the while he wondered if he was too late....

CHAPTER TWENTY-FIVE

Laura and Charlie stared at each other for the longest moment. Laura touched his hand. "I always wanted a son."

Charlie's words were full of emotion, "And I've always wanted a mother."

They hugged, and Laura held him at arm's length. "You definitely didn't get any of my features." He was tall and had cold black hair and eyes. It was obviously he was Italian. "You are so handsome!" She beamed.

"Thank you...mom." He grinned. "I got my father's looks, but not his demeanor. I can't do the things he does. I won't ever..." His voice softened, "It doesn't matter. We will both be dead soon." His eyes watered. "We won't even get the time to know each other."

"Stop it, Charlie." Laura suddenly remembered why they were there. "I won't lose you and my daughter to that horrible man." Her eyes darted around the room. "We have to come up with a plan."

"Do you really think my dad was serious about having you kill me, his own son?" Charlie asked.

Laura couldn't lie to him. "Unfortunately, I believe he would. He's a very spiteful man."

"I don't know my dad very well, I guess. I've heard rumors, but I didn't want to believe them."

Laura wanted to reach out and hold her son and promise him that everything would be all right. She thought of all the years she missed out on him growing up. She knew Paul's mother, Gracie Gallo. She wasn't the best role model for Charlie, but she was sure glad it was her that raised him rather than Paul. Her heart ached, knowing that Charlie grew up thinking he didn't have a mom. *What kind of father tells that to a kid? The same father that would rather have his son dead if he didn't kill his own mom.* "That's it," she said aloud.

"What?" Charlie asked puzzled.

\*\*\*

After a short while they pulled into the long driveway, leading up to Paul's colossal house. Chandy squeezed her eyes shut in disbelief. She wished this was all just one big nightmare, but she knew it was useless. She could only pray that her mom was still alive.

She decided not to volunteer to get out of the car. But it didn't matter—Paul jumped out and hurriedly rushed around the car to open the door for her. "Out," he growled.

She knew she could scream or fight and kick him— *but why.* In the long run, he would get her in the house one way or another.

"You want to see your mom one last time, don't you?" Paul asked coldly.

"Please, I beg you not to hurt her." After hearing Paul's last words, Chandy eagerly followed him into the house. The two vile men followed close behind them.

Doris was standing by the entrance to the front room, looking more nervous than usual, Chandy noticed. Her eyes met Paul's, "I have not left this spot, Boss." She eyed the gun on the end table. "She wouldn't have made it out alive if she tried." She grinned uncertainly.

"Good job, Doris." He held out his hand. "The key."

Doris hesitated briefly and then placed the skeleton key in his extended hand.

Without any hesitation, Paul unlocked the door.

Chandy reluctantly followed Paul into the room. She wasn't sure what she expected to see but she hoped more than anything that her mother would be there unharmed.

"Mom!" She was sitting awkwardly on the edge of the velour couch. Chandy ran to her and threw her arms around her slender neck. "Are you okay?" She immediately noticed the cut on her lip and the bruise across her cheeks. She nervously traced her finger around the bruise. "Did he do this to you?" Chandy's mouth dropped.

"I'm okay, baby girl." Laura squeezed her tightly. "Thank God, you are okay."

Chandy's eyes narrowed as she glanced over at Charlie who seemed to be lost in his own little world, playing with his cell phone. "Charlie?"

He glanced up at her. "Yeah?" His eyes were vacant and cold. He immediately shifted his eyes back toward his phone.

Chandy's heart plummeted. She was so disappointed. She thought he might have had some compassion toward her mother since he knew what it was like not to have a mom.

"Okay, baby girl, time is up," Paul said, mocking Laura.

"No," Chandy said. "I'm not leaving my mom."

"I don't think you want to witness this," Paul said callously. He motioned to the door. "Now go on—get up to your room."

"No!" Chandy planted herself next to her mother. "I won't go."

"Suit yourself." He turned toward Charlie, "You have had time to think about your options, have you changed your mind?"

Charlie held up his cell phone before setting it on the table. "You know, Dad, you forgot I had my cell phone. I could have easily called the police to come and help us. But after I thought about it, I couldn't do that to you. You are all I have. You are all I have ever known besides grandma. This woman may have given birth to me..."

Chandy gasped loudly. "What?"

Charlie continued, "But she means nothing to me. Nothing at all!" He shrugged his shoulders. "And I don't want to die, myself."

Chandy shook her head in disbelief. She couldn't believe her ears. She had really thought Charlie was different from his father. She'd been so excited to find out she had a brother. Now he was acting just like her so-called father. She was infuriated but also confused. "Is my mom your mom too?" She looked anxiously toward her mom for the truth and her mother nodded.

"See, we could have been one big happy family." Paul grinned ruthlessly. "That is if your mother hadn't gotten greedy and decided she should have you all to yourself."

Chandy was truly baffled. "But why do you have Charlie?"

"If you wish to stay in the room, young lady, you need to shut your mouth," Paul growled. "I have other things to do today. I have already lost sleep over this mess you have created." He turned his attention back to Charlie. "So, you decided to shoot her yourself?"

"Yes, Sir," Charlie said.

"What the hell!" Chandy felt her mother gently squeeze her leg, but she didn't care; she wasn't scared of this man that claims to be her biological father. *Over my dead body will I let anyone shoot my mother right in front of me.* "No one is shooting anybody unless they want to shoot through me to do it." Chandy jumped to her feet and stood in front of her mother as if to shield her from any bullets.

Annoyed, Paul yelled toward his men. "Wes, Ratty, get this brat the fuck out of the way."

His men each grabbed one of Chandy's arm and pulled her toward the door. Chandy screamed and tried to pull away but could not get lose from their firm hold. She watched in horror as Paul edged closer to her mother. She screamed loudly, but it was suddenly silenced by a cloth jammed in her mouth. She fought the scumbags with every ounce of strength that she had, but it was useless. Her eyes filled with tears as she watched the horrible scene unfold in front of her.

Paul jerked the gun from his jacket and held it in the air. "I'm going to ask you one time and one time only, son—are you sure you can do this?" He eyed Charlie with the coldest look she'd ever seen.

Charlie eyes met his father's as he reached for the gun. "I'm positive. I want to make you proud of me, Dad."

Laura quickly spoke up. "No, Charlie, you don't want to do this. Let your father do it. Don't be like him. You don't want to go to jail for the rest of your life." She pleaded loudly, "Please, Paul, just let me and Chandy go. We will leave you and your son alone and never bother you again. Please, I beg you."

Paul grinned. "Not a chance."

Charlie took the gun from his father.

Omigod, Chandy couldn't bear the thought of her mother being shot right in front of her and by her own brother too. Her mind raced. She spat the cloth out of her mouth onto the floor. She had to somehow convince Paul not to kill her mother. She pleaded, "Paul, I mean, Dad, please don't have Charlie shoot her!" Chandy's voice cracked nervously as her words rushed out, "I will live here forever with you. And I will marry whoever you want me to." She glanced toward her mom. "And unlike her, I will never run off like she did. I promise you that. Please, Dad, just let her go!" Chandy could tell the word *Dad* had caused him to hesitate but not for very long. "Go ahead, Son, today you become a real Gallo!"

"No," Chandy screamed. She twisted and fought like hell to pull her arms free from the men.

"Get up," Paul nonchalantly told Laura. He glanced one last time toward Chandy. "This is your last chance to leave the room."

"No," she screamed again. "Please, Dad, don't." Her sobs were growing uncontrollable as she continued to fight to get loose.

Charlie held the gun up to Laura's head. "Good bye, Mother. I'm sorry we don't have time to get to know each other, but we don't.... so, adios."

"Charlie, don't do this!" Laura pleaded.

Suddenly, Laura fell to the floor, and Charlie spun around with the gun aimed toward his father. "I will not kill my own mother. The mother that you lied to me about!"

"Charlie, my boy, what the hell are you doing?" Paul asked casually. "Don't you know my men here will kill you."

Charlie didn't break his stance or his stare. "But I will shoot you first!"

"Not today, son!" Paul jerked another pistol from his jacket and fired a solo shot at Charlie arm.

Chandy screamed as Charlie's gun fell to the floor, and he clutched his bloody arm in pain.

Paul shook his head. "See Charlie, I knew you didn't have it in you. I'm afraid you didn't take after my side of the family at all. And you will never be a true Gallo." He aimed the gun toward Laura. "You're a disappointment, Charlie. I will show you how a real Gallo has to survive in this world!"

Chandy screamed, "No!"

From nowhere, Doris pushed through the door pointing a small silver pistol at Paul. "No," she yelled. "I won't let you shed any more blood!" She glanced at Charlie. "Especially your own son. How could you do that to him? He is all I have left." A solo tear slid down her cheek.

Chandy was speechless. Everything was happening so fast.

"Doris, don't do something stupid," Paul said puzzled. "You don't want to die this way. You have been with me for years."

Her eyes stayed glue to Charlie. "Can't you see, he needs a doctor or he going to bleed to death!" She shook her head. "I never could have a child. I've always pretended that Charlie was my boy. He means the world to me and he is all I have left, Boss! I refuse to let you kill him, not while I am still breathing."

"Stupid woman! We can take care of that." He swung his gun toward her, but Doris was faster with the trigger. The shot rang out and hit Paul in the chest. He crumbled to the ground clinching his bloody jacket. "Kill her," he muttered weakly toward his men.

Chandy couldn't control her loud sobs. She had never witnessed any brutally of any kind.

She jumped as she heard a loud voice, speaking over a megaphone, "Paul Gallo, this is Sam Rivers with the FBI. We have your place surrounded. I advise you to come out slowly with your hands up along with the rest of your men."

For the first time, Chandy saw fear in Paul's eyes as he looked defeated.

Ratty eagerly lied his gun down. "I'm done. I would never kill Doris, not even for you, Boss."

Paul eyes narrowed. "This is all your fault, bitch," he growled at Laura." He rocked back and forth on his knees in pain.

As soon as the men had released Chandy, she'd ran toward her mother, who was trying to stop the blood gushing out of Charlies' arm.

Wes dropped his gun also and followed Ratty outside. They both held their arms above their heads.

Doris rushed to Charlie's side to see if she could help Laura stop the bleeding.

Within minutes, the house was full of FBI men, and Paul lifeless body was placed on a stretcher.

Chandy cryed. "It's over, right? He won't bother us ever again, will he?"

"It's okay, baby girl," Laura said softly.

Charlie glanced up toward her. "I'm sorry, Chandy for making you think I was going to kill your mom. Me and your mom planned it. We knew it was the only way we could get my dad to hand me the gun. It was the only chance I had to save your mother—*I mean our mother*." He glanced down at his arm. "Sorry our plan didn't work, and I couldn't outwit my father!"

Chandy massaged his good arm. "It's okay. I'm just so thankful it was all a phony set-up."

"Dad," Chandy spilled more tears as Scott came running in.

"They wouldn't let me come in until it was all clear. I was going nuts out there." He hugged Chandy. "Are you okay?"

"I'm fine and looks who else is fine." She beamed proudly as she pointed toward her mom and smiled from ear to ear.

He winked at Laura. "Yeah, you are going to hear an earful soon!" He hugged her tightly. "But not now."

Laura quickly introduced Charlie to Scott and explained to him how he was Chandy's twin that she hadn't ever known about.

"Wow, unbelievable," Scott said, shaking his head. He thanked Charlie for the bravery he had shone to save his mom and sister.

Ambulance attendee was motioning to Laura that he needed to take over. He called his other attendee for a stretcher.

Sam called across the room toward Scott, "You guys need to get out of here."

"Okay, we are leaving," Scott yelled back. "Thanks, Sam, for everything! I owe you!"

As Chandy followed her mom and dad toward the door, Sam quickly rushed over to them. "I just got a call, Paul Gallo died on the way to the hospital. I just thought I'd let you know."

"Wow, okay thanks again, Sam." Scott shook his hand.

"No problem, buddy." He patted Scott on the back before crossing back to the others.

Scott quickly told them how Sam Rivers was going to keep mom's name out of the whole bust. As far as they were concerned they didn't know anything about her.

The attendee had confirmed that Charlie would be fine, but they needed to take him on a stretcher. Chandy leaned over Charlie as she walked next to the stretcher, "What are you going to do now?" she asked. She knew he had heard Sam say that his dad had died.

"I don't know. I can't believe he is really dead." He paused. "The worst part is I don't even feel sad. I never knew he was so evil. I thought it was just a bunch of rumors."

"I'm sorry." She truly felt bad for him. She had been blessed to grow up with their mother and a truly awesome father, and he had been left with this horrible man and a grandmother which she knew nothing about.

Charlie glanced around at his surroundings. "I guess the estate would legally be mine, but I'm sure it is all dirty money. I don't want to be any part of my dad's life. I have no desire to be part of a Mafia of any kind." He reached for Doris's hand. "You should have this place. You deserve it more for all the years you had to put up with him."

Doris eyes filled with tears as she squeezed Charlie's hand.

Laura whispered. "Come back to Missouri and live with us," she said sincerely.

Chandy chimed in, "Yes, please. You would love it there!"

Scott nodded. "And I would be thrilled to have another man in the house." He rolled his eyes toward the women and winked.

"Seriously!" Laura said. "Walk away from this life, right now, and never ever look back. You are my son, and I've missed out on the first seventeen years of your life. I don't want to miss out on any more of your life."

Charlie's eyes lit up, and Chandy was sure she'd seen tears glistening in them. "Okay, I will," he agreed.

Chandy's heart was filled with love for this brother that she had briefly known. She grinned happily, "At least there was one good thing that came out of all of this—*I have a brother.*"

"Correction, you have a twin brother." Charlie teased.

"I know...bizarre, right...since we don't even look alike." Chandy's heart was filled with joy. Although she'd just experience the worst time of her life, she now was sharing the best day ever with her own brother. And she had her mother back. She didn't think life could be better. *Yeah, it could,* she thought, *back in Missouri far away from this city.* She hurriedly followed her mom and dad to the ambulance as they lifted Charlie into it. "We will see you at the hospital," she told Charlie. She gave her mom and dad a powerful hug before climbing into the taxi.

Visions of her home and the woods surrounding it excited her. And Kyle...she could hardly wait to see him! No one would ever believe the nightmare she had just gone through, so there was no need to tell anyone. They would have to make up a good story about their mother coming home, but dad had promised that his friend, Sam Rivers, would work all the details out for them.

She squeezed her eyes shut and quickly thanked God for hearing her prayers. She suddenly giggled.

"What are you laughing about?" her dad asked.

"I was thinking about our dogs and that make me think of the movie *Wizard of Oz* and Dorothy and Toto. I remember when I was gagged and tied up at that disgusting motel, I kept looking at my red tennis shoes and thinking, "There's no place like home."

Her mom and dad chuckled. He mom wrapped her arm around Chandy's shoulder and squeezed. Chandy had never felt so much love than that very moment.

She knew from this day forward life would always be good. She didn't remember ever being this happy! *And there really is no place like home,* she thought silently.


The End